Voyages

Voyages

Peter Najarian

Pantheon Books
A Division of Random House
New York

ISBN: 0–394–46917–8

Library of Congress Catalog Card
Number: 70–147802

Manufactured in the United States
of America by The Colonial
Press Inc., Clinton, Massachusetts

First Edition

For Zaroohe Najarian

My friend, I am going to tell you the story of my life . . . and if it were only the story of my life I think I would not tell it; for what is one man that he should make much of his winters, even when they bend him like a heavy snow? So many other men have lived and shall live that story, to be grass upon the hills.

BLACK ELK SPEAKS

Voyages

Hemingway in the Mayo Clinic and Faulkner home all day in Oxford: my heroes are falling. Old men bullshitting for the magazines. Disgraced. Veins worming out of their hands. Home together in my country where my father suffered. They must not die without honor as if they were defeated immigrants, their lips twisted and their hands curled and sunk into dead loins. Die, but not with grotesque mouths, death relieving a weary nurse's aide from emptying their bedpans. Not with the ashen face of Lincoln in the picture before his death, with the frozen eyes of a paralytic.

Once they went fishing together. I want to have been there, to have ridden piggyback upon their shoulders. I want to sit near them, around a fire late at night, hear them talk of things I never found in the books. Drunk, they would click tin cups and toast the past, toast each other, and finally my generation:

"A toast to Aram's generation."

Too late: if I went to them now I'd be just another sycophant. I must leave them alone. I must grow up. Everybody's dying. Frost was blinded at the President's inauguration. No one reads Wolfe anymore.

Highpoint Avenue was clean on Memorial Day (1961) and only an infrequent bus broke the silence. One boy was up early to make sure his mother would iron his scout uniform for the parade; another boy would also go to the parade and shoot paper clips at the powdered thighs of majorettes. Neither of them associated the occasion with the cemetery.

Alone now in her kitchen Melina leaned out of the window, level with the Empire State Building across the river, and tugged at the washline heavy with billowing sheets. With the window open the kitchen smelled blue and white of the clouds and the breeze. After the laundry was pulled in and piled like a crumpled sail on the small couch, the *sedir,* by the window, she folded it and then sat down and put her glasses on and darned my socks. Then she made coffee, set cheese and *choreg* and olives on the table, and then walked through the railroad rooms and nudged my bed. My room was dark but for a thin light streaming through the window that faced the alley.

"Hadeh, ehleeh, oosheh," she said happily—Comon, get up, it's late.

She went back to the kitchen and sat on the *sedir,* and from the sewing basket on the radiator cover she

4

took a pair of large scissors and, expertly holding the blades instead of the handles, cut her flat dull nails as low as she could. When finished she picked the crescent scraps from her lap and collected them in her palm. A thousand years before, her ancestor would have hid them in a holy place, a crack in a church wall, a pillar of a house, or a hollow tree because the severed portions of his body would be wanted at his resurrection, and if he had not saved them he would have to hunt for them on the great day. Melina knew nothing of that and dumped them in an ashtray on the radiator cover. When I was a boy I piled my comic books on that cover, always keeping those I liked least at the bottom of the stacks which would dry and fade from the heat. My father read them all in his last seven years; he sat on the *sedir* next to the window, the cane at his side, his hand in his crotch, and read through my childhood from Plastic Man to Archie Andrews. I still read them for a few years after he died and then I don't know what happened to them. There were at least a few hundred. I always wondered what he thought of them.

The morning sun made me squint as I came into the kitchen.

"*Pari louys,* Baron," my mother said—Good morning, Sir.

"Good morning, Ma."

She got up to reheat the coffee. I washed in the sink and dried my face with the towel that was folded over the wringers of the washing machine.

"You came home late last night," she said. She never asked me where I went but she wanted to know if I enjoyed myself.

"I went out," I said. "I had a nice time."

"Good."

She poured my coffee, put the Silex back on the stove, and then put bowls of soaked vine leaves and meat-and-rice filling on the table and sat across from me. I dunked a piece of *choreg* in my coffee and nibbled it with feta cheese and black wrinkled olives. On an old board white and clean with the texture of driftwood she smoothed a vine leaf and then put a pinch of filling on it and rolled it into a small neat cylinder that looked like a green Tootsie Roll. It was called *derev dolma* in Armenian and *yaprak sarmah* in Turkish. I used to be ashamed of my mother's food when I was a child. I used to yell at her: how come we don't eat steak and potatoes like everybody else? She had strong hands, red and blunt like a butcher's. She sat with her elbows wide, her shoulders loose, like Picasso's picture of Gertrude Stein.

"What did you do last night, Ma?"

"I went to Sahagian's."

"Did you have a nice time?"

"We talked."

"About what?"

"They're going to the cemetery today, too. We talked about their dead and about your father."

"Did they talk about how intelligent he was as they always do?"

"They talked about how he wasted it."

"Like me?"

She sprinkled some water on the filling and with her wrist wiped a hair from her forehead.

"They talked about you, too," she finally said.

"They said it would be easy for you to be a doctor or a lawyer."

"Do you want me to be a doctor or a lawyer?"

"You can be whatever you want."

"But you don't want me to be like him."

"I never told him what to do."

"But you wanted to."

"No."

"Yes."

"Why?"

"Because he was weak."

"Everyone respected him."

"But he let you support him."

"It was the *Depression*." She pronounced it like an Armenian word, accenting the last syllable.

"It wasn't the Depression, Ma. You were stronger than he and he let you support him."

"No."

"But he was weak, wasn't he?"

"Why do you say that?"

"Why are you afraid to say so?"

"Why do you want me to tell you that?"

"Because he was."

"He was your father."

"Do you want me to be like my father, Ma?"

"He was your father. Don't you want to be like him?"

My mother and I walked down Twenty-sixth Street and at last I was proud of her, was no longer ashamed of the short and fat illiterate immigrant peasant, was honored to walk beside her, the last of the immigrants. The cemetery was on the other side of West Hoboken, near Secaucus which was the public dumping ground. Twenty-sixth was a slum street; the Puerto Ricans had settled in and most of the Italians and Syrians and Armenians had died or moved north. But the tenements were the same and in the brightness of the morning they were more than slums; the sun checkered with their fire escapes, hydrants leapfrogged with garbage cans, scully squares on the sidewalk, box-ball chalk on the pavement; Twenty-*Spic* Street, the last community, there'd be no more immigrants, everyone was on Welfare. We passed Central Avenue, once called The Dardanelles, where young foreigners carried knives, wore long scimitar sideburns, played backgammon and cards in a little store without a sign, its dusty windows covered with old velvet green drapes. Now it was a Spanish cafe. It too would disappear. From Hudson Boulevard we heard the final dying sounds of the parade as it marched toward City Hall, little Spic kids watching it, eyes wide to a procession of home guard soldiers, ears inflated with the drum and trumpet noise of Sousa music, flags waving to the pageant of an American ceremony, and they joined in with the same spirit they saluted the flag every morning and sang *Land where our fathers died.* . . .

Most of the graves were filled with Americans, their tombstones sunk below the level of the grass in the original grounds. The Armenians were buried in the new grounds added during the Depression. My father's grave was one of the latest, the wide space around it still unoccupied. Buried eleven years already. Only bones left. Hair and nails scattered in his clothes. Blood, drained and emptied down a sink, somewhere in the sea now, reduced to its elements, floating, floating, perhaps eastward again.

My mother crossed herself but she did not cry. I did not cry either nor did I cross myself. Engraved on the gray marble slab were the letters of his name that seemed to belong to someone else: Petrus Tomasian 1893–1950.

"What are you thinking, Ma?"

"He has a nice place. Nice and clean."

"Yes."

"You like it?"

"It's nice."

"What are you thinking?"

"I want to go."

"You didn't even make a cross yet."

I lit a cigarette and flipped the match in the path.

"You're just like him," she said. "He didn't believe in that either."

"Let's go, Ma."

"All right. Get some flowers and then we'll leave."

I walked awkwardly to the hothouse, not knowing whether I should shortcut by stepping on the graves.

"Deghas," my mother called—Son.

From where I stood she looked noble and dignified over her husband's grave.

"Deghas, get a flag, too."

> then he was twenty-one. He could
> say it, himself and his cousin,
> juxtaposed not against the
> wilderness but against the tamed
> land which was to have been his
> heritage. . . .
>
> from *The Bear*
> —William Faulkner

I wore faded work shirts and old faded corduroys and walked slightly bowlegged in an awkward swagger. I brushed my teeth with salt, shaved with a straight razor, did calisthenics every morning, and never slept more than seven hours a night. But no matter how hard I tried to discipline myself I felt doomed to be worthless, dull and ugly.

I was kicked out of college for stealing books. I went back to live with my mother for a while and then decided to move to the Village and find a job. Yero, my brother, called me a crazy bastard and said I could live on my own when I got married like he did but I was stupid to move out for no reason at all. My mother was unhappy about it but said I should do whatever would make me happy and if moving out would do it then I should move out. Yero drove me in his car, the back seat loaded with my clothes, radio, lamp, bedding, typewriter and food my mother had stuffed into jars. When we came out of the tunnel I tried to give him directions but he said he'd be damned if I knew the city as good as he did and I was a stupid son of a bitch for wanting to live in such a filthy fucking place. We took the West Side Highway and turned off at the Nineteenth Street Exit and when he saw the house he called me an idiot, said he shit in better places and that I was probably going to live with a bunch of beatniks. He said:

"Just watch you don't get the clap."

I didn't answer.

He helped me bring the stuff in, up a small flight of stairs and down a long dark hall, and when I opened the door he said:

"Jesus Christ, Aram, my bathroom is bigger than this."

"You'll tell Momma I live in a nice place?"

"You don't think I'll tell her the truth?"

"It's not so bad. It has a big window."

"Sure, but where the fuck is the walls?"

"It's only seven bucks a week."

"You know, sometimes I think you got brains up your ass."

"Well, thanks for bringing me here anyway."

"You sure you know what you're doing?"

"Sure. I like it."

He left shaking his head.

And so, *starting across the river from where I was born, well-begotten, and rais'd by a perfect mother, I did strike up for a New World:* oranges and bananas on the dusty window-sill, peanut butter and baked beans and a lamp I made in sixth-grade shop class next to the hot plate on the chest of drawers; I typed my journal sitting on the edge of the bed with the typewriter on a box—there was no room for a chair; I asked my journal: is masturbation my fault, America's fault, whose fault a virgin and lonely? cockroaches in the bathroom crawling over the cracked mirror in the morning when I shaved, the radiator moaning at night as I lay in bed and listened to it go on and on—it wasn't the radiator: when I first moved in I listened to it moan for two nights before I realized it wasn't the radiator but a woman on the other side of the wall and never having heard such a sound come from a human being before I thought she was sick at first until I heard her boyfriend's voice, I was that dumb because why? who, what could I blame for my ear next to the wall on the other side of which a young couple made love naked while I was naked? was I diseased? why didn't I join the army instead of living alone, stealing books stuffed in my pants, walking out of stores as if with my finger up my ass, piling under my bed three hundred books cached for the future as if someday I would read them all from Aristotle to Zeno? No, it was not for a library but because books were the only things worth stealing and one had to steal something, either steal or beg but somehow get something for nothing. Why? Why couldn't I be law-abiding instead? Whose fault was my life? I never was a beatnik in heart or style yet one Sunday visiting my mother across the river someone I knew from high school saw me with a mustache and knew I lived in the Village and put mustache and Village together and asked me: Hey, Aram, are you a beatnik now? I didn't know what to say, said Yes, lied and told the truth, for what was I or wasn't outside of my little room the size of a toilet? Who were

12

my people? Who was the young man on a bench in Sheridan Square or St. Mark's or Washington Square Park wearing dark glasses and rags, his face lost to the sky, whom I felt related to not by nation or by blood or by creed or by drug but shame as I was ashamed of masturbation, and pride as I was proud of all the books I had stolen and would never read? I found out Norman Mailer lived in my neighborhood and one night I ran up and down the streets yelling: Norman! Norman! not knowing what I would have done if he answered, yet needing someone desperately who knew the way in the new world which was a community only as long as one never used the first person plural. Yet who was Norman Mailer? What could he have told me, poor man? And could he have defended me before a judge if I were ever caught stealing? Could he have proved I was innocent, working for a bank that I instinctively hated and was justified in hating, running around Wall Street with a black messenger's bag I used for stealing not only books but whatever I felt like having for supper, innocent in elevators full of girls who pressed against me and obliterated my face with their tits, bobbing bold as brass, saying: touch it, dare to touch it, just once, touch this tit and we'll cut your balls off! That was punishment enough for stealing tuna fish I ate alone at night, sitting on the edge of my bed, waiting for a beautiful girl to open the door and lie beside me, waiting, waiting, until I could wait no more and masturbated like a flagellant —that was punishment enough. I had thought that a girl would save me. But there were no girls in my world, the new world, there were only women. And through my yellow eyes the difference was that a girl was someone to love and a woman was someone to fuck and only fuck, a biology lab instructor with slides of human sperm, a housewife who came out for the milk and paper naked under a short kimono, a dentist's nurse with my elbow in her crotch, a creature naked under her dress on humid afternoons in the subway. She was one of the assistant managers in the bank and I met her in the lounge when she came down for coffee. She didn't wear lipstick or high heels and she combed her hair like a cheerleader and sat with her legs apart and with her clothes on she did have a girl's body. But she was forty-six years old and I was not only afraid but embarrassed. So she took me gradually, inviting me first for a drink on a Sunday afternoon and then to dinner on a Tuesday night in her studio apartment in Brooklyn Heights where she lived alone since her last divorce, an expensive place off the esplanade with a doorman who said: Yes, please? I said: Miss Mildred Van Ness, please. He pressed the button beside her name: Woman: red hands, old breath, waiting for me with steak and artichoke and candles. Waiting with after-dinner cognac. Waiting until when finally she kissed me I told her I didn't know how to take her clothes off. Don't worry about it, she said and shut the light and went to the bathroom and let me undress alone. Later she asked me what was wrong and I said she made me feel like a girl, taking me that way and leading me to bed. But she said I had plenty of time to be hard-nosed and predatory, should consider myself lucky to have it oozed out of me with such a festoon of sex as she could offer, all young men should learn of it from such experienced loins. *Reaming* she called it. And I discovered the odor: prime-

14

val, exuding as if from the lips of something coelenter-
ate, viscous and deep: on the floor, in the bathtub,
astraddle the bowl, vertically, backwards, upside down
and sideways, with wine and whipped cream: until all
that remained at dawn when I walked bowlegged past
the doorman was fatigue and the memory of her hands.
My seed was futile inside her. I was ashamed of her. I
was ashamed of self-abuse again when I went back for
more and waited for her to return from a nightclub with
one of those men old enough to be my father, waited by
the fence of the esplanade, the small lights of Hoboken
glimmering across the bay, waited for my old woman.
And they brought her back to me, *beaux* she called them,
one a president of a bank, another a captain of a Caribbean liner, and yet another twenty-grand-a-year man,
all cinquanters trying to get her pants down. She
dropped them only for me and I was ashamed of her
and her limp thighs. Yet she wouldn't have believed it;
she had life by the balls, she said, and nothing was
going to drag her down again. In the half-light of her
bedlamp I watched her face change back to the girl of
thirty years before, the young girl in the Depression,
sweet as stolen fruit from a poor farmer who couldn't
sell it anyway. I loved her then. Too late. I lost my vir-
ginity to a middle-aged woman. The last time I saw her
I gave her a copy of Van Gogh prints I had stolen especially for her as a going-away present—she liked Van
Gogh, poor man—and I left her place at dawn, shook
hands with the doorman and told him I'd never see him
again. From outside a delicatessen up the street I stole a
bag of fresh bagels and a quart of milk just delivered as
if especially for my breakfast. Perhaps the new world

was especially for the hobo, perhaps it was only the hobo who could make his way in the new world. I took the ferry to Staten Island and started hitchhiking at the Turnpike entrance. Her withered thighs wide open, I entered the mainland of my country with a Yale man just finished with his exams and rushing back to his girl-friend in Memphis. We drove crazy from New Jersey to Tennessee in less than a day, zooming inside the Whore with a big Oldsmobile ninety miles an hour. He was a tall stupid handsome young man, very straight, who did not want to I'm sure, because he was very gentle and meek, but could not help making me feel like an immi-grant kid whenever we stopped to eat; it was impossible to find decent food on the highways of America, yet my Yale friend with magnanimous indifference ordered any old shit without reservation or complaint, while I, who had trouble enough paying for food in general, was so fussy and awkward that I could order nothing but pie and ice-cream as if I did not know enough English to order anything else. Yet I liked him, had to steal some-thing from him to keep us level or I would have hated him, so when we stopped at his white house, while his mother fixed us breakfast, I stole a book from his fa-ther's library, shoved it in my duffel bag, and said so long, thanks a lot for the ride: she was my country as well as his. But she wasn't, didn't seem to be anyone's, just dry endless land indifferent to anyone's claim: any-one could fuck her for a price. If you wanted her. But she was aging fast. I wandered up and down and across her and came out of her ass in Los Angeles, rats in the palm trees, oil derricks on the beaches, banks that looked like churches and churches that looked like

16

banks. She had life by the balls she said and nothing
was going to drag her down. In the half-light of dusk I
watched her hills change back to the country she must
have been a century before, sweet as stolen fruit from a
people who would have shared it freely. Somewhere in
Kansas I wanted to stop. I was tired. I hadn't slept for
two nights and I was beginning to feel delirious. It was
about three o'clock in the morning and no rides. I
walked about five miles and came to a motel-restaurant.
I washed my feet in the sink in the restroom, shaved,
brushed my teeth, changed my socks and underwear
and once again I loved America for its cleanliness, its
lavatories as white as Eisenhower, its wall-to-wall carpeting as neat as George Washington in that picture
with his bottom half washed away. She was immaculate, a young sweet girl behind the counter. Her name
was Genia but it just as well could have been Jane, Jane
of my primer stories of Dick and Jane and their little
dog Spot, and when she asked me what I wanted I fell
in love with her all over again, and I wanted her, I
wanted my country back. She said:

"You're from New Jersey?"

I said:

"Hmmm."

"Are you going back there?"

I said:

"Hmmm . . . I mean, I don't know."

And I told myself I would stay in Kansas, find a job,
court her, kiss her, play with her: for couldn't we be
happy, wasn't it possible? I said:

"May I have another cup of coffee?"

"That's your fifth cup already."

"Hmmm."

And I asked myself why not.

"How come you don't know?" she said.

"Don't know what?"

"If you're going back or not?"

Why not ask her?

"Will you marry me?"

And she stared at me with that familiar expression, half of fear and half of indignation.

My brother had a different father but we both looked very much like our mother, talked, walked and moved alike. But the difference was obvious whenever he gave me advice:

"Go back to school, get a degree, get a job, and join the crowd. You had enough of this 'being different' bullshit."

The degree was like passing a civil service examination: I was stamped *approved*. And I took a job no one else wanted, the only kind worth taking, affording enough opportunity to lie and forge and steal from my country and repay it with some honesty, for I found no other way to live in America except by stealth. I became a Welfare Investigator in Harlem. I went through a door marked PERSONNEL ONLY. I unbuttoned my collar and loosened my tie as if I were important. I was money for a hundred families, I, who felt that I would never have a child of my own.

Pending Social Study: Priscilla Lee, Puerto Rican, fair skin, green eyes, long auburn hair, considers herself Negro and Harlem her home. "Why should I want to live anywhere else? I love Harlem, I love the Apollo, I love St. Nicholas Avenue, and I love my mother (Mrs. Mary Lee). No, I don't want to move." Priscilla is an amiable girl, a good dancer, and very intelligent (I.Q. 150). She lives with Mrs. Lee in a large room sharing cooking privileges and toilet facilities with two other families in the apartment. Her real name is Dolores Minoso. She was born in New York City fourteen years ago to a Miss Carmen Minoso. The name of her father is unknown. At the age of five weeks she was abandoned on the doorstep of Mrs. Mary Lee. Mrs. Mary Lee is a huge, robust, tobacco-chewing, septuagenarian, childless widow. She has supported herself and Priscilla with her Social Security check supplemented by Welfare. She is at present on this investigator's caseload. Priscilla has hitherto never been mentioned in the case records because previous investigators could not explain her existence. She was never legally adopted and no one could account for how Mrs. Lee got on all these years without an additional allowance. Mrs. Lee, however, has managed well. But now it is imperative that Priscilla be included in the budget because she is pregnant. The putative father of the yet unborn child is George Washington. George Washington is fifteen years old, attends school, is unemployed and unable to contribute anything to Priscilla. He lives with his grandparents who are also on this investigator's caseload. The whereabouts of his parents are unknown. Priscilla is unsure whether she will marry him or not. Nevertheless she is eager to have the child and looks forward to being a mother and continuing school.

My supervisor said in her mellifluous Negro English:

"Mister To-mas-ian, take this here off my desk and send it to Child Welfare. This girl is ob-viously neglected. It's a BCW case. They'll find her a foster home and put the baby up for a-doption."

"She doesn't need a foster home. All she needs is a bigger place with Mary Lee. After she has the baby she can go back to school and Mary Lee can care for it during the day."

My supervisor sighed, rubbed her eyes, and shifted in her chair as if she were constipated with her twenty-three years of civil service. She said:

"Now how you going to es-tablish that? You got to prove she got a good home now, don't you know? How you going to prove that? Mary Lee is seventy-eight years old. She ain't even a le-gal guardian. And this here Priscilla ain't but fourteen. Now what you think that's going to look like on paper?"

She was right. Everything was done on paper. You were born on paper and you died on paper; you married, fucked, and divorced on paper, had children on paper, drove your car, drank, went to school, worked and didn't work on paper, were success and failure on paper; you were nothing without paper, no one, a hermit, a hobo. If you wanted to account for yourself, justify yourself, you had to do it on paper in one form or another—license, permit, tax, certificate, degree—stamped and approved, a matter of references, qualifications, addresses, and dates. So then the best way to survive was to learn the shyster's trade, a few numbers here and a few names there and lots of lies all over the place. And it was my job to lie for Mary Lee and Priscilla.

But I forged my supervisor's signature for the last time. I was caught and fired and never found out what happened to those two people who wanted a home together. A home together. It was like trying to turn the pyramid, Novus Ordo Seclorum, upside down lightly upon the nose of a seal—with *the seal's wide spindrift gaze toward paradise.* America was one vast foster home.

Harlem: deep in the nook of Central Park and Morningside Park, turning a volte-face from the western sun and St. John's Church high on Morningside Hill, incarcerated, huddled in the corner of the island like a prisoner with her knees drawn to her breasts.

Suddenly I was above and out of it. Climbing Morningside I looked up to the rump of the richest and largest church in America. An archangel, like a scavenger bird on the back of a hippopotamus, stared over the valley. Inside, the church was empty, its vast echoing space dumb and useless.

Columbia across the street: I passed the medical school's library, then Butler Library; carved on the lintel of Carpenter Library the names of Greek writers were disgraceful and disgusting.

Broadway was bleak and desolate. High gray hotels and apartments like slag deposits. A dirty, ugly, humped-over bum sneaked out of an alley, touched me, and whispered:

"Excuse me, Sir, but . . ."

I said:

"Leave me alone."

And I walked away, my fingers in my pocket jingling my change. If I were poor, if I were poor enough, then no one, not even a bum could ask me for anything. America asked too much of me and I wanted to escape her, as an orphan from an orphanage.

I evaded Times Square by turning right on Forty-eighth Street and I passed the building where my father used to work. I stopped for a moment and stared at the people on the block, the same kind of people he must have seen every day on his way to and from that work which never made him any money; he dressed like them, read the same papers, spoke the same language with an accent: I wondered what he thought of them, what he thought of American people.

In the terminal the busses coughed gas, snorted, purred and panted as if they were alive. My father had his stroke on the floor of a bus as it was going through the tunnel; the other passengers had loosened his clothes and looked for identification in his pockets.

In Weehawken, sweeping high above the waterfront into the Palisades, I looked quickly to catch a final view across the river: Manhattan, silent and clean, golden by the glare of the low sun; she looked innocent from a distance.

High in an ILGWU factory Melina sang inaudibly, yet in counterpoint to the ululation of machines, a chanteuse among the International Ladies. The Ladies, twenty fat old immigrants, sat with their hands buried in chiffon and their feet smothered in dust, making Mademoiselle's dresses. They each sewed and sang with their own rhythms. A cacophony of foreign melodies and stertorous machines. The last of the fat old ladies, the good old mothers. Grandmothers—factory workers. Melina finished her dress and called it a day. And forty years. In which the hours were shortened, the pay increased, and the machines improved, and it became even more absurd.

Late in the afternoon she walked home behind a long and majestic shadow. In Bakalian's Oriental-American grocery she bought two pounds of heavy-cut bulghur, a dozen dried eggplant skins, two ounces of coriander, and peppers, squash, okra and stringbeans. Next door in the Italian bakery she bought Syrian bread, the kind with a hole in the middle. Carrying the heavy brown paper bag against her chest as she would a baby, she struggled up the block with food for her child, me, watching from the window.

Take it back, Ma, the bundle and my life, take it back for refund.

I met her at the door, took the bag, and climbed ahead of her.

"Aram," she said, "you need a haircut."

"I'm bald, Ma, I don't need a haircut."

"So you're bald. Your father was bald and his head was always neat."

"I'm not my father, Ma."

"You're his son. Why don't you let me see you look like a gentleman once in a while?"

"A haircut costs too much money."

"Perishan, perishan" she said, a lamentation for the poor.

23

We ate in silence while I looked at the evening paper. When she saw I wasn't really reading it but just turning the pages she said:

"Are you going out tonight?"

"No."

"Why not?"

"I have nowhere to go."

She tried to smile. She said:

"How did you become different?"

"I'm not different, Ma."

"Yes," she said. And then in English:

"You not normal."

"Why?"

"You're always unhappy. Why don't you go to a head-doctor?"

"What's he going to do for me, Ma?"

"He'll give you some pills or something. Something to clean you out."

From the kitchen the aisle, like in a railroad car, passed two bedrooms and opened to the final room called the *parlor;* long and yellow dust-filled shafts of light extended into the room from a fat sun sinking behind the marshes in Secaucus. It was like an eighteenth century drawing room, but twice removed from elegance by lack of money and incongruence: a delicate silver tray on a cheap coffee table; crystal candle holders on the mantel of a false fireplace; plastic flowers between organdy curtains; intricate lace doilies on bad

24

imitation Chippendale; a bumpy elephant-shaped sofa covered with a floral chintz; and everything confused with the oriental rug, maroon and blue with tiny crimson birds and deer.

Melina poured pistachio nuts into the silver tray and set beside it a dish of *lokum,* a jar of raisins, walnuts, and salted chee-chee beans. A woman called Automobile Zabel sat in the corner, a shawl draped over her shoulders; it was not cold but the old say drafts are everywhere and she sat with her hands clenched in her lap as if she were shivering. She said:

"Didn't your landlord turn the heat on yet?"

"No," Melina said, "not yet."

"You should complain."

"It does no good."

"Maybe you should move."

"How am I going to move, Zabel?"

"Aram should help you."

"Hoos!" Melina whispered. "He's in the kitchen. Don't talk again about him not working. He'll be leaving soon again."

"Don't *hoos* me, my girl. Am I supposed to whisper when he's around? What's he doing home at night anyway?"

"I don't know. He looks like he's reading."

"He reads too much. He should get married."

She was called Automobile because for years after she arrived in America she would never cross the street alone she was so afraid of cars. Many of the immigrants carried English nicknames. There was once an old man called Cockroach Oskan because he slept on the floor and kept pieces of stale bread in his lint-filled pockets

25

and walked all the way from West Hoboken to Fort Lee once just to save a nickel carfare. Another was called Gangster Levon because he was hot-tempered. There was Shoeshine Krikor who wore patent leather, Pinochle Nishan, Brooklyn Ruben, and so on. Automobile Zabel had come to America in 1928 from France. Her husband was killed by the Turks in 1910. She escaped from the massacre in 1915 and went to France where she met another Armenian there who was in the French Army. She married him and had another child and then he was killed in 1917. She lived with her daughter's family in Weehawken. She didn't get along with her son-in-law; his own mother complained of living alone.

Two other women, Shamir and Nevart, arrived together and Melina put their coats on the bed. Shamir sat on the sofa with the weight of a boulder; she was built like the trunk of an old oak swollen with tumors; her breasts were as big as watermelons and her ass like a giant pumpkin; the springs of the sofa made just one quick squeak and died under her bulk. She was called *Medzmayr*—Grandmother, though she had no children in America. Her fine long iron-gray hair was simply plaited behind her neck; the tan skin of her face looked tough like leather, but when you kissed it was as soft as a flower, and her soft brown eyes, deep within wrinkles, seemed protective and all-knowing. During the massacre she was raped by a Turk who fell in love with her and brought her back to his village. She lived with him and their two babies for three years and then he died. After his death she tried to escape with her children, made her way toward Beirut, but at the border the

26

Turks seized the two children and expelled her alone to Beirut. She remarried there and came to America in 1925. Her husband died of cancer during the Depression. She lived alone in a furnished room in the house of her husband's cousins.

Nevart—translated Rose—entered sprightly, and in her movements were still hints of the agile and flirtatious girl she once was in the *vorpanotz*, the orphanage in Beirut where she first met Melina. Her hair, decorously waved behind her gold earrings where once in youth it curled in black ringlets, was now the color of artificial pearl. Unlike the others she went regularly to a beauty parlor, was the only one of the group whose husband survived and prospered after the war. During the massacre, when the gates of Diarbekir were opened to the Chechens on horseback, she was sitting half-conscious beside her dead mother. A brave had lifted her up on his horse and then she was in his tent and for the next three years wandered with his tribe, a Chechen girl gathering firewood. Until one day when a Syrian merchant who spoke Armenian took pity on her and helped her escape to Aleppo where she joined other refugees and came to the orphanage at Beirut. She was brought to America in 1920 to marry a man she had never met before. Her two daughters were both married and lived in the Catskills. She kept home for her husband whom she never loved.

Each of the women took a corner: Shamir and Nevart by the windows, Zabel on the sofa, and Melina straight in a chair ready to go and come from the kitchen with fruit and coffee. They did not wait to start talking. No one lacked anything to say; no one distrusted another enough to be silent, nor could they afford to distrust one another. They had to stay together; for how many were left who spoke the same language? They had been together now for more than a generation and stayed together with only one simple rule: no silence. If, as a child, one had to choose between the men in the parlor and the women in the kitchen, in those days when the husbands and wives were together and there were enough of them around, and one had to choose whether to sit in the parlor with the men who sat drunk, head in hand, eyelids heavy, just listening to an oud solo or playing backgammon slowly with grunts and groans, or to sit with the women in the kitchen cracking squash seeds with front teeth and drinking rosewater, then a bored child would choose the kitchen where the gossip was, the dissertations, lamentations, arguments, and free-for-alls on rising prices and other people's lives. They talked with the energy of schoolgirls in an ice-cream parlor. But the boys were gone. They were in the parlor now. The kitchen was empty. The men were dead. Or dying. Crippled. Or silent. They endured, sipped thick coffee from delicate china held by heavy fingers, said in unison: I don't play bingo, I don't like television, what else is there when I'm alone and my children have moved; I talk to myself in the supermarket, a boy yelling at me: Whatsamatta lady can't you read don't squeeze the fruit! How do I know it's good? It's good lady don't worry it's good! Should I trust you? Trust me lady it's good fruit!

It was rotten fruit. They escaped a massacre and married their brothers in a land of refuge only to live

28

alone in small rooms waiting for the once a week or
once a month when they might see each other and talk.
What was left to talk about?

This President's eyes look tired.

They're Irish eyes.

But he's young.

He has too much worry.

What does he worry about?

You ask?

He must worry about something.

Not about us.

All the Irish have sad eyes. It's their religion.

I like his eyes. That's why I voted for him.

Yes, they're gentle.

They're all the same garbage. Even Roosevelt.

Roosevelt was a cripple. He knew what suffering
was.

This one has a bad back.

They say he's a hero.

We're all heroes. I'm a hero. You're a hero. So
what?

He's all right. I like his eyes.

Did you vote for him?

I don't vote.

I don't vote either. Are there any Armenians to vote
for?

I voted. I'm a citizen. Why shouldn't I vote?

You can't even read.

Do those who read know any better? I liked his eyes.

They're Irish eyes. He worries about his own kind.

We're all Americans.

Oh, we're American now?

Why not? Our children were born here.

You want them to marry Americans?

Why not? What's the difference?

Just because they're born here doesn't mean they're Americans.

Who's American anyway?

Anyone with money. You can do anything you want here with money.

I have money but I'm still alone.

Saturday morning smells of bleach and soap, fried onions, boiling tomatoes, cold dry air through the open window. The wringer-washer whirls back and forth. Water crashes in the sink. Melina says:

"*Hadee yallah, Deghas, oosheh, oosheh.*"—It's late, my son, get up.

Get up! Get up! to the morning commandment: Thou shalt do something!

Ominous faces in the cracks of the ceiling: Aristotle defining happiness for his son, Nicomachus: . . . not a condition but a form of activity good in and of and for itself. But can one get paid for it?

The hollow eyes of chimney pots, their cowls shaped like Ku Klux Klan, stare across the roofs. On a fire escape a boy with a bee-bee gun shoots *ping!* at a pariah cat.

"These are Indian names in our neighborhood," my fourth-grade teacher once said and wrote on the blackboard: *Weehawken, Hackensack, Passaic, Moonachie, Man-*

hattan. I was an Indian then, adventuring strange streets with bow and arrow of sumac branches, hiding behind elephant boulders, shooting at cars on the ramp to the Lincoln Tunnel. Or I was a white man shooting at Indians. It did not matter who I was then from one day to the next because finally I was everyone in history. Spread-eagle at the monument, high on the Palisades, where Burr shot Hamilton dead, I once touched George Washington Bridge with my left hand and the Statue of Liberty with my right: the *Queen Mary* in pier across the Hudson was a toy boat in my gutter puddle: I built the Chrysler, RCA, and Empire State Buildings with my erector set. It was once my country, a child's country.

And then? From Queequeg and Daniel Boone I became no one, an amanuensis for an immigrant.

Vahan's tailor shop was a few blocks from the Hamilton Monument in Weehawken. I hurried there for my weekly visit. I had to piss and there were no public lavatories around, none on any of the streets in America—building them could have been a WPA project but now the Works Progress Administration was gone.

Van's Valet—the name suggested by a friend who thought it would stimulate business—was a dilapidated shop Vahan kept to make his last years more dignified than they would have been if he went to live with his son in the suburbs. I was there when the name was suggested. Vahan had said in English:

"Van's Valet? Sound nice; sure, vhy not? Vhat it mean?

"Valet means *baharzdur*," I said.

"No," he said, "I'm not that."

"What's that word?" the friend asked me.

"Servant."

"No," he said to Vahan. "It means tailor."

"Ah, yes," Vahan said. "But Van, vhat's Van?"

"You know," the friend said, "like Van Johnson."

"Who?"

"The movie star."

"Oh, movie star. Now I'm a movie star?"

Fortunately the name was unsuccessful, for Vahan didn't really want business stimulated; he wouldn't have been able to handle it if it were. He wanted only a place to live and some work to do. But when I tried to get him to change the name he seemed to like it:

"I'm a movie star now," he kept saying.

He was on a bench sewing a pair of pants. The bell tinkled.

"Hello, Baron Vahan."

"Hello, Aram," he said, his voice weary as if it came all the way up from his toes, echoing through a skeleton.

The shop was alive with clothes, puffs of dust like tumbleweed rolling tenderly across the bare wooden floor, water dripping from a steaming boiler into a rusty coffee can full of floating matches and cigarette butts, and the odor of benzine stinging my nostrils.

Vahan slept on a cot in the back and shared the small greasy stove with cockroaches. The toilet outside was a small closet of unpainted brick, the stained brown bowl smelling of Lysol flushed with a long chain from a high wooden box. A very pleasant piss.

"Inch bes es?" I said—How are you?

32

He nodded his bald wrinkled head, lumpish like clay molded by a child, the sunken cheeks formed by the heel of the child's hand, the eyes by deep thumb marks, the nose by a pinch of the fingers, and the mouth by a crooked line of the nail. He put the pants down and lit a cigarette and smoked it delicately, holding it in reverse with the gnarled thumb and middle finger of his big hand, veins swollen under a dappled thin membrane of skin, huge husky yellow nails so hard he had to cut them with shears. He was eighty years old and I loved him very much and I had been waiting for him to die for a long time—every time he moved I watched anxiously as if he might cave in and crumble like a heap of clothes piled on the floor.

"Should we continue your story?"

"Yes," he said and walked behind the counter and got his manuscript and my translation. He sat in a chair by his old sewing machine, the kind that worked with a foot pedal. I read what I had written before:

MY MEMOIRS OF THE FRENCH VOLUNTEER ARMY,
by Sergeant Vahan Vahanian.

I was born on February 25, 1883, in Hahvav, a suburb of Balu, but when I was a small boy my mother and I moved to Kharpet and at the college at Kharpet I received my schooling.

In the spring of 1906 my mother and I went to live in Rumania with my father and brother who were political exiles. In 1910 I came to America. In the fall of 1917 thirty-seven of us Armenian young men in America volunteered for the French army, and then we went to Cyprus where we trained for three months and waited anxiously. I and five others were promoted sergeants. In May of 1918 we sailed from Cyprus to Port Said and from there we went by train to the front at Palestine. We were stationed at a little town, Megidiya, for a month and then our platoon was sent to the first line of the front with two machine guns. For thirty-six hours without stopping we fought the Turkish and German troops. We took the Arara Hill. The enemy retreated only to be pursued by the English on horseback coming from the rear lines. We recovered our wounded and dead and captured our share of the prisoners. Our wounded: 105; our dead: 75. That was the battle of Arara Hill. Our wounded were rushed back to the rear lines. We built a cemetery on the crest of the hill and buried our dead side by side. Two of the boys brought broken wood from a nearby village and we made crosses. Vagharshag Vartabed, who now lives in Providence, Rhode Island, performed the ceremony. Then we returned to the main lines.

The bell tinkled and a customer walked in with some clothes. I gave the customer a pink receipt and he left.

"Okay, Baron Vahan," you just buried your dead and Vagharshag Vartabed from Providence, Rhode Island, performed the ceremony.

"Yes," he said, and found his place.

"Don't you want to say anything more?" I said.

"What do you mean, more?"

"About the battle and the fighting?"

"I said everything."

"Okay, then, let's continue."

He had to read the manuscript because it was written in Armenian script which I didn't understand, and we progressed slowly.

We rested for one week and then went on the road to Haifa. After three days marching we reached the Jordan River and there we rested for one day, each of us washing in turn. The next morning we were back on the road; we reached Haifa late at night. We stayed for two days. The next day we came to Acra. Three-quarters of Acra is built on the Mediterranean shore and the rest is on dry land surrounded by high walls with only one gate. We pitched our tents outside the walls, and we stayed for one week. While we were here we heard that four forces took Beirut. Most of the people in Acra were Arabs but there were some Turks left and plenty of Armenian refugees. Four of us were allowed leave to enter the city: myself and my friends, Arsen Boyajian who is still alive and lives near me now, Souren Yaldizian who is now living somewhere in Watertown, Massachusetts, and Antranig Dadaian who is now dead. The four of us went through the gate and looked for Armenians. We came to a French Catholic church. There were plenty of Armenians there. Most of them were from Cilicia. A Cilician boy told us there was a house nearby in which an Armenian girl was kept. An Arab landlord was keeping her for his son. "What's the girl's name?" I asked the boy. "Annahid," he said. "Does she have a mother and father?" I said. He said, "Her mother and father and my mother and father and many other mothers and fathers were murdered at Dortyol; the children were brought here and I was among them, but the Arabs took some of us like Annahid." Arsen Boyajian turned to me and said, "Ser-

geant Vahan, since you speak Arabic we should go to this landlord and get the girl out." So the four of us and the boy went to the Arab's house. I knocked and an old woman opened the door. I said to her, "This boy tells me my sister is in this house; I want to see her." The woman denied there was a girl in the house. I said, "Old woman, if you don't get her, this house will be burning soon." The old woman called inside, "Ahya, come down." A very pretty girl with Armenian eyes came down and looked at us meekly. "Ahya," the old woman said, "do you recognize this man?" The girl stared at me and before she could say no I said, "Annahid, don't you recognize me? I'm your brother." Her eyes became wide. "What happened to my mother and father?" she said. I said, "Don't you remember I went to America? Now I have come back to rescue you from here." But the girl said "No, you are not my brother. What happened to my mother and father?" Just then an Arab man came walking down the street and entered the house. The old woman explained the situation to him and he said, "Soldier, the girl does not know you. Why don't you go away." I grabbed him by his collar; I said, "Listen, Arab, I came to this god-forsaken place to free my people; if you don't release this girl your house will be burning and you will be burning with it." The Arab looked into my eyes; he said, "Ahya, you can go with these men if you want." I said to him, "Don't call her Ahya; her name is Annahid." Annahid packed her things and came back with us to the camp where she ate and slept well. I later heard that she got married and came to America.

The bell tinkled and another customer walked in but this time Vahan got up. I put the manuscript and the translation into the drawer under the counter.

"No more today?" he said.

36

"No, I have to go."

He went back to his bench.

"Do you think it can be printed?" he said.

"I don't know."

"That's all right. As long as my grandchildren can read it someday."

"Why?"

"You ask why? They're my children's children, no? They're Armenian, no?"

"Yes, they're Armenian."

"They should know what it means, no?"

"Yes."

"Do you want coffee?"

"No. But tell me something."

"What, my child?"

"Why didn't my father join the Volunteers?"

"I don't know, Sweetheart; I never asked him."

"Was he afraid?"

"I don't know. It doesn't matter."

"What was he like?"

"What do you mean?"

"What kind of man was he?"

"He was a very good man, a very sweet man."

"Was he anything else?"

"He was a smart man."

"You sound like my mother."

"What do you want to know, my child?"

"I don't know. Anything. What were his politics?"

"He didn't have any politics. But if he were in the old country he would have been a Hunchak. All his family were Hunchaks."

"Were you a Hunchak?"

"No, I had no politics."

"What was your family?"

"My father was a Dashnak."

"Did you ever argue politics with my father?"

"No, why should we argue politics in America? In America we were only Armenians."

Said in the first person plural; yet what did it mean, Armenian? From what inbred generations did he become a big nose, deep eyes, heavy eyebrows? Urartu swallowed by Armen. By Mede. By Greek. By Mongol. By Arab. Until in America he became me, a dead end, speaking Hoboken English: *I wuz nuttin* in the third person: singular: the son of Petrus and Melina was not a man, only looked like one because he was bald; he loped down the street like a camel, ruminant, long-necked, humpbacked, mopish and purblind, his long nose leading the rest of his body; furtively he stole glimpses of himself in the reflecting store windows, a ridiculous khaki figure frightfully resembling someone real, wandering streets frightfully familiar, streets once belonging to someone real, someone adventuring and claiming that curb, that hydrant, that pole for his own for the rest of his life as if like a pioneer who could choose anywhere he wandered for his own, the child once real who knew himself without asking had the right to claim a home where he was born; he walked home by memory now, no longer privileged, climbed the stairs as if a visitor; he got the brown photographs from the musty closet, pored through the faces of the dead; he lowered the stale Bible from the shelf and read the dates: he was born, yes, underneath his father and his grandfather, and in the mirror he resembled someone, the same nose and eyes not of his father especially but of a people, yes: but when he looked close and hard and silent and tried to hold on to an image of the past, to some link with an ancestor, to keep balance with himself and the past, the nose slowly wavered, swelled into a tumor hiding itself beneath its own growth and the eyes saw not themselves but the vapid gaze of no one in particular, a vague vestigial face not even an apology for the generations descending from the high plateau where once Urartu girls opened their legs to Armens, their daughters fucked by Medes, semen starting its long journey downstream where Greeks came and Mongols came and Arabs came, to end nowhere in America, the struggle of ten thousand thousand pricks futile in America, ending in a bald sterile creature masturbating in the mirror.

My mother naked in her old age sat on the edge of the bathtub fat and abundant like a Renaissance nude, her skin quickly pink in a thick cloud of steam, and handed me the *keseh,* the itchy blue flax glove, and I rubbed her back as if with sandpaper, superficial epidermis peeling off into tiny black filaments she thought were dirt.

"Your back's not dirty, Ma."

"Rub it anyway, please," she said and sat hunched over hiding her pudenda with her hands. The communal bath was gone where once women, as in a seraglio, rubbed one another, later sat in burnous towels and gossiped eating grapefruit. Now only I was left to rub her back.

She came into the parlor in her burnous towel and watched the television with me for a while until I asked her if she liked it and she said no and went to bed.

I watched the late show and the late late show until I was tired enough to go to bed.

The most important mistake I ever made was to believe in God—*Asdvats Dada*—the father of my father who could make my father better. Every Sunday for the second five years of my life my mother handed me a nickel for *Asdvats Dada* who lived around the corner in a dark and golden place behind an altar smelling of burning perfume. I went early to be alone with Him leaving my own father in the kitchen as if I were his emissary. The old black wizened women were always there first, in front of the pew, whispering behind my back as I tiptoed down the aisle: *The son of Tomasian comes to pray for his father.* I hated them, their blasphemous stares in the back of my neck, as if it were they who prevented me from communicating over the candles and beyond the picture of a Mary and a Jesus baby. The old fat priest sat in his throne pretending not to notice when the nickel clanked in the metal box under the candles. I lit the candle and crossed myself one-two-three-four without the names and said *Please,* and said it again, and again, wanting to say it aloud, afraid of the black women listening, the fat priest listening, not only as if He were my God alone but as if what I had to ask Him were shameful: *Please make him better:* as if his illness were a punishment.

I believed in God as I believed in my country, that

concept to hold as I might hold my father were he not a cripple. And when he died and there was nothing left to pray for, God was useless and there was nothing left, nothing that was myself instead. Nothing remained but the ancient odor of incense, the calm color of tarnished brass, the dissonant chant of an old deacon swinging a thurible. Bones in a box; hair and nails scattered in the lining of his suit; blood somewhere in the sea.

My father?

Who art?

In high collar, small knot in a tight tie: posing as if a prince or a president: with rectitude before the black-cowled photographer.

Petrus Tomasian, the youngest child: he was born by the Tigris in 1893 in Diarbekir, a walled city on an ancient caravan route from Baghdad to Constantinople. The city of Bekir the Invader, it was called Tigranakert in Armenian; the city of Tigranes, translated Richard, it was Dick's Town before the invasion. No real difference to a child: words like homes intertwined in the labyrinthine medley of Turks, Armenians, and Assyrians, where a child could skip across the flat tiled roofs from home to home, spying down into open courtyards at veiled women and Christian women, innocently invading anyone's privacy . . . until, very early, he learned the word *odar*—stranger.

He was a happy child with red hair and flushed freckled cheeks, who trembled when he laughed and stammered in his speech—his father said it was because he was ambidextrous, could not tell the difference between right and left. His father, Aram, an old carpenter: strong chin, stained white mustache like long oxhorns; gnarled hairy forearm, thick wrist, thick knuckled fist tight on a sweat-smooth hammer handle, nails between his lips: at night he smoked his narghile with slow pleasure, head in his hand, listening to an oud

42

solo, *taxim,* aracq glimmering on a table, ten thousand memories buried beneath his wrinkled eyes.

They ate on the floor, everyone from one pot, dipping bread into one of his mother's multifarious stews— *zahd.* She cooked on an open fire in the back: he never saw her stop moving, drawing water from a well, he never saw her away from water: she was always smiling, even to herself after dinner bent over embroidery, listening to his older brothers and sister: Boghos' legs crossed under his oud and Garabed in counterpoint with his zither, and his sister Annah sang low sweet words the color of honey. In a house of black stone, cool and smooth, he had a home—*Doon*—for seven years: *Doon* echoed from his contented belly: *Doon* the odor of tobacco and charcoal, coriander and garlic: *Doon* of shish kebab in warm summer evenings, his older brothers turning skewers of cubed meat and vegetables over embers red and black like the dusk sky, sizzling from dripping juice, a fat red sun on the horizon enjoyed by both Turk and Armenian: and *Doon* in the winter feasts of lamb and quince, later stored in deep jars, eaten cold, the sweet white fat congealed with dry meat and chunks of quince like candy: *Doon* in his first seven years before a new century.

Then Annah married: in white: her groom, Stepan, led her away on a donkey, bells on its collar. Then with their baby, Hagop, they went to America because Stepan was running away from the army. Her green eyes, long auburn hair, odor of lemon, gone: Annah who would kiss him sweetly as his old mother never could, gone: she kissed his eyes, his ears, his cheeks, she kissed him on the mouth: they all stood by the wagon by the gates of the city and she kissed them all, hard, harder, not with apology but resignation as if to say: *It's not my fault, don't blame me.* He never blamed her for going to America: many were going: *Ah-mehr-icah:* the sound of it seemed so solemn and final, as if everyone had to go there sooner or later. They watched the back of the wagon disappear into the horizon, westward toward Aleppo.

In his second seven years he was all hands and discovery: in sacred nooks and crannies, under the rug, behind a book, in back of a closet, he hid the treasure of his adventures: a yellow tooth, an amber button, bits of glass: buried in his home to protect him: he kept a ritual guard on his talismans, lest anyone should find and remove them.

When his eyes and fingers developed a harmony, his brothers, both architects, gave him paper and pencils, and he started drawing: by the river, by the gates, on the roofs: oxen and donkeys, dragons and phantoms: on Sunday afternoons he copied the pictures in the church: the history of Armenia was incidental and he gleaned it in the meanwhile, never thought of the river or the hills beyond or the city itself as Turkey or one-time Armenia, but was content to draw indifferent to names.

At night he heard his brothers argue with the Dashnaks, the nationalists, who wanted their country back.

"No more nations!" his brothers said. "Haven't they caused enough pain?"

44

And he learned from his Socialist brothers that he lived under foreign rule but that all nations as nations were foreign.

The third seven years were shock: not only in his own body and the upheaval in his loins, but the whole world seized, foaming at the mouth: when the notice came that he would be taken into the army, the Turkish army, his brothers decided he should leave: Annah wrote: *Yes, come quick!*

And it was done, quick as a line drawn by ruler, demarcating one part of his life from another, like a swift line by his father sawing wood in half with one-two-three strokes and it was done: *Doon* gone: as if it never, not ever, had any foundation at all but was built upon ephemeral odors, moments of touch, a gossamer web of happiness: his mother packed his bag with dry meat and *choreg,* sewed money in the lining of his jacket, and suddenly he was looking at them all as if to say: *Please don't blame me, it's not my fault.*

"Write to us," Boghos said. "Long letters."

"And send your sketches," Garabed said.

They both smiled broadly, black mustaches wide and rising, as if they were happy.

His mother and father did not move.

The wagon master yelled departure in Turkish: *Hadee yallah!*

Vomit and delirium on the high seas.

They found a louse in his hair on Ellis Island and shaved it all off. It never grew back the same and he was bald by eighteen.

Annah lived in a strange place which smelled like a machine: her eyes were tired: she kissed him politely.

He learned the history of America by the stone faces on its money: with grave monotony the same little eyes stared from every dollar, the same frightening mute was engraved on every number. For his citizenship papers he learned the pledge, of liege to sovereign, the pawn of his fathers for the mummy faces of doom. An ominous eyeball beamed from the point of a new secular pyramid. He had left his drawings behind, dragons and birds, scarabs and deer, his childhood left behind with the destiny he once played with knucklebones, fortune dice flipped upon that intricate rug in his father's house.

There were two hundred Armenians in West Hoboken before the war: they built a church and a bathhouse and once a month rented a Swiss Town Hall for music, dance, and drama—*Hantess.* Sunday afternoons they trolleyed to the Palisades and picnicked by the river; they played backgammon and cards in a *khavah* at night . . . and they waited, and they saved money to bring the others over: they started all over. Most of them had brought their wool and their spices with them: after three hundred years the New World was stone, the green mildewed, the marrowbone sucked dry.

He fell into bed beside his small nephew whose

cherub face was almost a woman's. He needed one. Someone in the *khavah* mentioned a bordello in Jersey City. His first whore smiled a gold tooth. Then she asked him if he were a Jew.

"You look like a Jew."

How should he answer: when he said no he felt as if he had betrayed someone.

"I don't fuck Jews," she said.

And he fucked her, went in unto his first American whore, deceiving her loins and betraying his birthright, for he was a Jew, he wasn't one of her people.

Fortune wears the face of money: he needed a job to follow the kismet of his hands: through an Armenian jeweler from Istanbul he found work in New York and sat apprentice to a silversmith on Forty-seventh Street. On the ferry, ghosting into the morning fog, his hands over the railing, slow water flowed in rhythm to memory: would he ever see his family again, what magic carpet would bring them all together again? Annah had not forgotten but could not afford to hold on to the past and her own family tied her down: it was his prerogative to write back, to send money back for them to come over. Boghos wrote back:

"We're too old to move, but maybe our children someday soon."

A year, two, three, swelling like carbuncles in some corner of the back, unseen, unfelt . . . until inflamed. On the ferry his sketchbooks filled with totemic rocks towering above a river: neither rocks nor river, unbeautiful, ignored and patronized, were part of the city or the people: he sketched them as one copies the icons of a strange religion.

Annah's husband died in 1914. He wrote back to let them know. His letter was never answered.

Time is blood: flesh sliced open in the sun. And the end of time is bone white: an ivory stillness.

What is the face of Charon?

One escaped, a boy, Carnig Sahagian, who remembered the day: his eyes were bold; there was no other way to stare at Petrus but like a judge who sentences the condemned with slow words.

"When the tide was down they ferried your brothers and the other resistance leaders across the river. Into Obolos Valley. Where they were killed by sword. They were not buried. Soon the gates opened and the Chechens came, screaming."

Vahan Vahanian told him about the French Volunteer Force: to kill Turks: to rescue the refugees: to go back for revenge. Vahanian's collar open, his knuckles white with fury: "What do you say, Petrus?"

Bones bleached in the sun, black mustaches wide and rising, each hair blown and scattered by indifferent scud: their wives raped, their children scattered across the desert, the old man and their mother dead by shock.

"What do you say, Petrus?"

Pieces of himself floating in the wind, the drawings he left behind, fumes of garlic and tobacco, oud and zither waves, the purl of charcoal in the breeze: honey

in the sand with the childhood he left behind and the
golden chattel of his mother's kitchen, hieroglyphic
brass, and all talismans, occult buttons and teeth, buried with the garbage: somewhere between the River
Kura and the Caspian Sea, Ecbatana and the Cilician
Taurus.

"What do you say, Petrus?"
You look like a Jew—I don't fuck Jews.

On the ferry through dawn his hands feel old: at the
war's end he's a quarter of a century gone, bald—the
final remnant of a hooknosed race. Woodrow Wilson at
Versailles draws a circle on a map; Armenia independ-
ent again after two and a half millennia, and the Dashnaks are jubilant. It lasts for one year, then the treaty of
Brest-Litovsk erases the line and it's finally over, a dead
land, no more nations; America will be the last nation,
the dump of refugees, dreg of all that blood.

"They'll be coming back," Annah said. "Vahanian
and Yaldizian and the other soldiers."

Her lips were dry: at thirty-eight, her husband dead
and her children too old to kiss and fondle, she already
spoke with the cynical voice of a matriarch.

"They'll bring the girls with them."

Hagop let his mother take care of the details.

But Petrus told his sister he did not want a wife.

She wrote to Yaldizian in Beirut and ordered one
wife for her son and slipped a small photograph of him
into the envelope.

Petrus moved out and found a room around the corner.

Write it on ice, my amanuensis: I remember more than I know, and imagination is yet more than memory. My father is a broken voice. And my mother always wears a kerchief and never stands still. And my brother is Everyman, *neither this one nor that. My head is full of odd remnants; my eyes are frozen, out of focus: I see everything at once and nothing in particular.*

A donkey is most real: his hoary ears frame one quick scene: I'm on his back in a field by our house and I'm calling to my mother, Doo-dee! Doo-dee! *That was how Turkish children said* Mama. *But we were not Turkish. Our food was Turkish, our music, our tongue, but my mother did not wear a veil. I sat in a cart behind an ox when we left our home in Adana: the road was full of Armenians: then the ox was gone and my big brother, Yerevan, carried me on his shoulders, my legs around his neck. One morning my mother told me not to go near my father and baby brother who were dead together at the side of the road. We left them behind. One morning everybody rushed to get back on the road to reach some point up ahead, but a bug in my ear, or maybe an infection? had made me sick so my mother and Yerevan had to stay behind with me. A bug in my ear: I give it to you now, my son, if you believe in destiny: all those who panicked were killed, were swallowed and burned in a ditch: read the writing on my forehead: I survived.*

My brother was a young man, I suppose maybe sixteen, seventeen? He was an artist like your father. Do you smile? I dream a voice: "Melina, if you'll sit still I'll draw your picture." I don't remember what happened to him. Somewhere, one day, he disappeared.

I think my mother was a stern woman: in the haze of memory I see blue eyes—they were probably brown but as they move toward me through the years they change color and she stands taller than anyone else, she smiles with her lips closed, her hands are flat and hard: one night we came upon the Turkish soldiers, a train, and other children; a scimitar hung from this soldier's belt —my mother told me to go with him, he would give me something to eat. I was her last child. I never saw her again, didn't cry for her until a long long time later when one night in the orphanage she came to me in a dream and I cried, cried loud enough for the nun to hear who came and sat with me until I fell asleep.

On the train some of us children were sick, and in a village they put six other girls and me in a room: read the writing on my forehead: all of the other six died.

(Ma!

Our big tits, our mustache stubble, garlic mouth— half your teeth gone milking our bones: may we eat orange peels from the gutter in prayer for the swollen belly of every tortured generation. Do we justify? Do we justify the burping, farting, snorting Turk, full of orgy: the fat Gestapo, the ecstatic bombadier? Take it back, Ma! To the lonely ziggurat in the desolate plain, under the flood sky, take it back, our hollow stare in the bright light as the sirens whine.)

I joined another train full of more girls and we came to a monastery in Beirut. There in the green hills above the city they shaved our heads, called us new names—my name was Lutvia— and made us pray to Allah: we were adopted by Mohammed. We

were from Adana, Urfa, Aintab, Damascus, Aleppo, Zeytoon
. . . we were familiar with the morning and evening muezzin
chants from the minarets in our hometowns—the mosques were
everywhere, the long trembling cry filled the sky in every village—
but none of us ever knew it had any meaning. And now we took
our slippers off and bowed our heads; now we were becoming
Moslem girls.

El-Hajj Malik El-Shabazz (Malcolm, we were almost brothers).

But the French came, then the English: Red Cross packages,
Lebanese nuns, a new flag. They gave our names back. The war
was ending. Yet we were still hungry.

There was a nun, Sister Sophia, who let me work in the
kitchen. I was her favorite, I guess, because I was especially
dumb. For extra bread I became her stupid unsuspecting chaperon,
and the three of us went walking, she and I and her Moslem
lover, whom I thought she was trying to convert. How hot she
must have been to use my innocence! It is said God keeps an eye on
idiots: like a donkey I wandered through the flowers while they
made love way over on the other side of the field. She should never
have married Christ: her face and hands were too beautiful, she
was too lovely to give Him the fruit of her youth, and she was
doomed to adultery. Poor woman, poor Everywoman, and poor
me. I did not know, did not want to know what happened under-
neath my dress. Nor what made that dark and hairy Moslem
different. But I was bound to discover, and better to learn of it
from her than anyone else, who taught me that the wife of Christ
could no more hide it under her habit than a belly dancer with her

beads. *The moon, the moon, my son, it wears the face of love and death: my time of the month had come and I was not a girl anymore. The day came when he left her crying on a rock; I had thought he hit her. Then she saw me step from behind the tree. "Please come here, Melina," she said in Armenian, but I did not move. "Please come to me, please," and she drew me to her breasts, held me tight, her tears on my face, her breasts full and firm under the cross, burning my cheeks, filling with strange warmth my own breasts which were then just beginning to bud: I felt her belly sink under my hand and rise again with her sobs; she smelled sweet, a young woman no more than twenty, half a girl, like me, and we stayed together huddled in the rocks, until— I didn't know why—it felt so good to hold her that I began to feel ashamed, and suddenly—and where the word came from I didn't know, as if it had nothing to do with my intelligence or education —said: "Do you love him?" She put her finger to my lips. Her eyes were full of him. In her eyes, as if I had been asleep until that moment, I slowly awakened to him, to all men, and to a mysterious pleasure so deep the loss of it could make even Beauty weep. A dark and hairy Moslem whom I once thought this side of ugliness had, through a tortured look in her eyes, slowly become desirable. That night she took me with her across the valley to a monastery where everything was stone silent. For two days we did nothing but pray and then I realized what she had in mind for me. My forehead, my son: I did not know if there was any kind of life better than one in a convent but on the third morning I woke before her, slipped away, and walked back to the orphanage, never to see her again. Years later when my turn came to curse the world, I remembered her and the stone silence of her final home, and envied her, her cold body wrapped in a coarse black wool.*

(Forgive me, Ma! For all the girls I hurt with my American dreams. For all the girls I made ugly and would not fuck more than twice, because I was *in love* with an actress, a waitress, a cheerleader, and a nun. Forgive me my locker-room criteria, my false manhood, my fashion bullshit. She had a big nose, the first girl who loved me, who cried when I left her because she had a big nose. She always rubbed her eyes to hide it, she always moved in her seat afraid to be seen in profile, her eyes were always downcast in shame. It's a long trip to her bedroom, long masturbating years of painted women in the mirror. It is a delicate room fringed with crinoline, curtained with muslin, covered with a jonquil rug, and the bed itself seems shy. I drop my pants in the corner; glancing at myself in the mirror I see a strange animal, a hairy barbarian amid flowers and lace. Suddenly she appears, with extravagant breasts, outrageous loins, and I'm afraid, Ma! she looks so ugly, her nose is too big. Forgive me, may the history of woman from the big-nosed Sumerian lady to the Congo women, Mongol women, and the lovely Indian women forgive me.)

Some families from the city offered foster homes and I went with an old Lebanese woman who called me Daughter. *At first her family was gentle, then they asked if I would help in the kitchen and in cleaning the house. After I learned all the chores they didn't ask anymore. I could have gone back to the orphanage but by then what difference did it make, orphan or servant?*

One of the sons in the house, Nubar was his name, was going to England with his new wife and they wanted me to come. I could not answer. Would England be any better?

Voyages

I was returning from the market with vegetables one afternoon when an old woman in the neighborhood called to me from her doorway: "Daughter" she said in Armenian, but I did not move. She came out onto the cobbles. "Isn't your name Melina?" I nodded yes. "Look," she said, handing me a newspaper of some kind. I told her I couldn't read. "Listen," she said, "Melina from Adana, my niece, daughter of Khosrof and my sister Turfanda." I shrugged; I did not know the names of my mother and father. "It is signed Ashod Aramian," she said, "with an address in Istanbul." I asked her what the paper was. "Names," she said, "They're trying to find their lost ones. You are Melina from the orphanage, aren't you?" I asked her to give me the paper to bring it back for Nubar to read. Yes, dim in my memory there was an uncle who came to our house, but I didn't tell the old woman: in those days I trusted no one as now in my old age in America I'm forced to trust everyone. Nubar wrote back to Istanbul and weeks later a thick letter came from my uncle who said that as soon as he could get the money he would leave for Beirut. In the letter he told me that my last name was Kasabian. I said it to myself in the mirror: Kasabian, Kasabian.

Nubar and his wife left. If it weren't for that old woman on the cobbles I think I would have gone with them: you were almost born in England, my son.

(Round around the little red bus—and may it survive, that last lovely toy of the empire—circles the Thames from Spitalfields to Kensington, Golders Green to Lambeth, from Coca-Cola to Kellogg's, Esso to Instant Maxwell House. America's colony will eat Kraft cheese on her rarebit. I tried to explain to a sixth form girl what it means to be an American but she couldn't get it out of her head that I wasn't a cowboy. They're washing St. Paul's, three hundred years black with industrial tuberculosis. Grosvenor Square is our embassy's front yard.)

I never saw my uncle. Everyone was going to America: soldiers were looking for girls to take back, and all the girls at the orphanage were blushing, whispering among themselves, not about the men—none of us knew what a man meant, the thought of sleeping with one seemed unnatural and dirty—but a home, and a home in America! Ah-mehr-ica: Ah-mehr: *it sounded so soft. I watched them leave, lips tight, afraid to say no to anything, stars in their eyes as if it were all a dream. It was Manooshag, fluttering, flowers in her hair, who brought her soldier to my house and introduced me to him, Krikor Yaldizian: Corporal Yaldizian with his belt below his belly, his eyes twinkled when he laughed, may he rest in peace. He showed me a picture of his cousin in America: Hagop, chest out like an aristocrat, a stiff arm and a cane, curls in his mustache. I told them that I had to stay in Beirut and wait for my uncle. And Yaldizian, that careless brain Yaldizian who lived with his eyes in his stomach may he rest in peace, said we could write to my uncle from America, send money to him and bring him over too. And I was that stupid to believe Manooshag's new big-bellied husband who wrote me down as his sister. Look, my son, at this passport picture: Melina Yaldizian, eyes empty like an idiot.*

(Don't be too hard with yourself, Ma: it's a typical orphanage face: everybody wears one for passports.)

March is colder than winter when spring is false. The water pipes were frozen in his house so he went to his sister's to shave. Annah and Hagop had gone to meet the boat, but they were too late. He was alone in the kitchen, shaving, when Yaldizian and the girl came. She seemed to resent the chair he offered her: she sat as if she were being punished while he and Yaldizian talked. When Annah and Hagop came back she was no different with them—lips tight, eyes hard. Yaldizian said:

"Melina, you couldn't stop talking on the boat and now you sit like stone."

"Leave her alone," Annah said. "Come, my daughter, come with me away from these men."

Hagop, not knowing what to do, let his mother take care of the girl until she was used to him.

Petrus watched his young nephew and Melina with bachelor eyes: Hagop seemed smug in his adoration of her, and she herself seemed deaf and dumb. He watched them carefully with the eyes of a man who once lived in another country—Annah at her wedding rode on a donkey, bells on its collar: could Annah's son and the strange girl from Adana make a home in America, have American children? Annah said to him:

"Now aren't you sorry we didn't get a girl for you? Look how beautiful she is: my son's bride."

It took a long time to join the Armenians in West Hoboken: just because I was Armenian didn't mean I was everybody's sister: first I had to be a wife and this takes longer than a day or a month or a year. Then, too, I was different. You think I don't understand when you say "I'm different, Ma, I'm not like other Americans"? Why do you think I don't tremble like other mothers when their sons go out with Italian or Irish girls? Petrus remembered his father's house and it meant everything to him, but what did it mean to me, ARMENIAN, except that it made me an orphan? And where was my uncle? Shooshanig Tamalian, you remember her, who lives on Highpoint Avenue, the lady with the lump in her throat—how do you say it: GOITER? She is over seventy now; last year she received a letter from Alexandria: her mother has finally found her, is alive today in Egypt, herself over ninety: what are they going to do, write to each other over the ocean? Maybe my uncle is alive today; am I going to take a plane to Istanbul? Hagop wrote him one letter telling him we had no money and Petrus wrote another one which said the same thing and after that we never heard from him again. You have cousins over there now, whatever this means.

(The world plays havoc in my head. Noise everywhere: next door the radio, upstairs they're dancing, downstairs they're laughing, and outside the dog, the dog, I will kill that damn dog someday. I'm not one for the commune, yet I cry for a home with my cousins, with my cousins. Everyone's my cousin, but it's too late. A head full of dust, knots in my throat, and a frenetic pelvis, I cry for bedlam: someone break me in half and smash my brain with a butcher's mallet: I'm crazy, Ma, I don't know how to live with people. Noise will kill me,

58

yet more than death I fear silence: no one answers in the ghost town of my nightmare: I cry to God and the moon says nothing. Come, my cousins, share my cookies—Go away, you eat too much, don't you know they cost sixty cents a dozen, my hard-earned money! But someone is always missing, there's always room for one more with still more soup in the pot, the thirteenth chair is infinitely vacant. What is the face of the monster that crawls behind me; what will save me from the monster in the closet? But I can't go to people whose noise will be my death. How did I once sleep with my cradle on top of a trolley? Where is sleep now at three o'clock in the morning with no sound but the hum in my head?)

The home was in the kitchen and the kitchen belonged to Annah, Annah BAHJEE—*she was* BAHJOH *by then, the venerable one—crow's feet twisting her green eyes, who took my brown envelope every Saturday, money I did not learn to hide for myself until nine years later when your brother was born. Two weeks after the boat docked I was in Barakat's factory six days a week —in those days a young wife was a servant until she had children and even then she had to compete with her husband's mother. There's something to be said for progress in America: nowadays let the old ladies mumble in the park.*

She made me wear a brassiere. My breasts were firm, not heavy like now, and I needed nothing to hold them high. But she said it was shameful to let anyone see them bob under my dress. I was hot under my dress and they knew it, mother and son, and made me feel ashamed so I could smile at no one, not even your father: in the nine years before your brother was born I never spoke to Petrus alone and yet there are still old women alive today who whisper that your brother is his son: viper women with forked tongues, so miserable who can blame them for their twisted teeth?

(It's not hard to understand adultery. Nations were born by rape. No one escapes the bastard's curse.)

I think the real difference between you and your brother, Yero, is not time but the kind of love that brought you into the world. It took many years to become a wife and then it was too late; I was forced to love Hagop and I never forgave him, poor boy, may he rest in peace. Fourteen years, count it on my forehead, twice as many years as your father was a cripple: Hagop loved Petrus, trusted him, respected him. But not once in seven years did he visit his crippled uncle, so deep did I wound him. He was not different from the photograph Yaldizian showed me in Beirut: chest out like an aristocrat, spats and a cane, curls in his mustache—he enjoyed a man's life. But he was his mother's son and it was her kitchen, not our home. And more khavah than kitchen after she started making aracq in the bathtub. She bought the still from Bogosian, the raisins she got wholesale from Nalbanian, and the anise from Tarzian the import man in Brooklyn. My eyes still burn when I remember the odor, like wine and vinegar. "Be quiet," she used to say when I yelled at her, "It's good money." I told her I could make enough so we could have a decent home, my first home, not a saloon where everyone from Paterson to Brooklyn congregated and gossiped, that gossip I hated all those years which when I divorced her son turned upon myself, Melina the whore. Maybe I was, maybe your mother was a whore, in mind if not body: what difference would it make? what meaning would it

60

change? "Mother!" I told her, "I'm unhappy." "You have no
right to be unhappy," she said, as if it were a man's privilege.
And she went into the grave a bootlegger with no life of her own
but a lonely son who never married again after I left him.

(I don't remember ever seeing my brother's father
except at the funeral. Strange to think of him as my first
cousin. But Annah Bahjee was always there at the window on one of my routes home from school. Someone
told me she was Yero's grandmother but that made no
sense so I never believed it: strange to think of her as my
aunt. She would call to me and ask me to buy her bread
and when I would bring it back she gave me a nickel,
an extraordinary, exorbitant tip in 1946. I don't remember her face; she died before I was in the second
grade. What a mess. What a hotch-potch of connec-
tions. I'll wager that somewhere in the synapse of stars
someday when this bloody web is disentangled I'll be related to Abraham Lincoln himself: and surely that
grisly ravaged mask descends from Ashurbanipal and
Hammurabi. Can't you tell me of the good old immigrant days, Ma, that I may see more than the broken
remnants of dissolute tribes, that Yero may be more my
brother than my second cousin? What of the paradise
welcome? Did the ships find no song, no beautiful
poem? Tell me *Hope,* Ma, the Passage to More Than
India.)

Zaroohe Sourian's husband, Levon, was known from here to
Boston for his oud: they kissed his bald head whenever he played:

61

even the dancers themselves would take dollars from their breasts and slip them behind his ear. Yet who knew that she was better than her husband? Her father and brother were master musicians in Antioch and she was playing since even before she went to school. But only in her father's house. And never in America. Because it was shameful; because she was better than her husband; because she was afraid. After she mentioned once that she knew a few chords I begged her to play for me but she always waved it away: "Only a few chords, Melina, that's all." Years passed until one day—I was pregnant with Yero at the time, swollen as an autumn melon—I waddled over to her house to spend the afternoon. She said, "Melina, tell me what you want, halvah, rah-jal, bastegh, lokum, *Hershey bar*, ice cream, anything and I will get it for you." And so I asked her to get her husband's oud from the closet and play for me. She was a tiny lady, my son, her feet hardly reached the floor if she sat on a high sofa, she was as delicate as china. Yes, it was shameful if the little sweat above her lip was shameful, her cheeks full and pink as she held that chubby oud in her lap as she would a baby, and stroked it, warmed up to it as if it were alive, slowly letting loose her frail fingers, until suddenly there, high in her apartment, above the trolley tracks, soup hissing in the kitchen, music, my son, not just to sing by or dance by but from deep inside her, buried beneath all those years in her husband's shadow, a taxim bubbling, flowing from her nimble fingers as if to form that long embroidery she had been weaving in her heart since her father and brother were murdered. And the tears down my face were not for her alone but my own loss and the nine years I never knew joy, never waved a tambourine above my head without shame as if there were something sinful in being happy, I had not learned how to be happy: where was kef for the orphan without a home, that dumb donkey who never learned how to love her husband because he was forced upon her?

Kef—orgy, the sacred rites of Bacchus; one learns *kef* in America from the bacchanal of Wop, Spic, and Nigger who mix it with blood; the slaves in the factories who stand half the day in steam and dust may get drunk every night and laugh from their bellies, but I still have a lot to learn; it's a long way to Dionysus through the slag canyons of quiet pilgrim bones. I listen to the concubine sing in the red-light nightclub and hear in her shrieks and throaty syllables, *yip-yip, lo-lah, lo-lah,* the wail of myriad babies left in the dust of screaming horsemen.)

Yero was born just before the Depression, when everyone had money, and everyone who had at one time or another bought aracq from Annah gathered around us and Annah's grandchild was covered with silver and lace, music, smoke, sugared almonds, sesame, kef: kef *for my baby, nine pounds bouncing: Hagop and Petrus, drunk eyes wet, arms around each other: Petrus said:*

"Atch-keet louys, Yegen"—*Light unto your eyes, my nephew.*

"Darose kezi," *Hagop said—May the same fortune be yours.*

Petrus held the baby between long gilded candles while the priest standing a step above them on the small altar mumbled and gestured through the baptismal rites; then in the little room at the side next to the kitchen where Sunday school met the priest lowered the child into a porcelain tub and pronounced him *Yerevan:* Edward in English.

His godchild looked like Melina: the same almond eyes, sensual lips. And what he felt for her slowly took form in the mysterious baby with the Cupid smile; in the following months he stared long and painfully into the cradle, drinking the image he never dared to face directly. He was in love with her. Maybe since that very moment the strange girl walked into his life, his face half soap, a bitter taste in his sex after ten strumpet years, and he watched her grow into *Melina* waving a tambourine over her head one warm afternoon of a picnic near Lake Hopatcong and suddenly found himself afraid to stare at her too long.

For a long time I could not conceive because there was something twisted inside me, the doctors said—but what do doctors know: Yero waited to be born until I was ready. And with the birth of my son I became a woman. When the Depression came I felt there was no more cause to hold on and was hopeful enough to think that nothing could get worse for anyone. I knew Petrus was in love with me—everytime I tried to talk to him alone he blushed and retreated—but it was not because of him I started to consider leaving Hagop. I wanted my self back. And I discovered a selfishness so ruthless I would not even listen to Yero say Papa *or fear taking him away from his father. I fought with Hagop without mercy. May my son forgive me, forgive me: I pushed* Papa *so far into rage one night he threw an iron at my head, and I used that against him. "It's your fault I'm leaving you," I said, and he stared at me as if I had just stabbed him.*

64

(You were forced to marry but not to split my brother's home. Yet where's blame in the spontaneous war between man and woman? Where's the family neither patriarchal nor matriarchal? The village belonged to Woman. But Atum created cities by masturbation, and Gilgamesh spurned Inanna. Finally Eve revenged her mother and sent us all to Hell. Where's Demeter in our Fatherland, Jehovah in our Motherland? Oh may the tide swallow their strife and with the sea-foam draw the white veil across their loins.)

Vosdanig Adoian had just finished law school around the time I decided to get a divorce. Though his mother and his wife's mother were part of Annah Bahjee's congregation and heard all the stories of my shameful ingratitude and disrespect, though I would be an outcast, a pariah, he said he would help me. I had known him since he was a boy working after school in Barakat's factory—he was about fourteen or fifteen then, and I used to catch him staring at me over his broom: he would sweep a little longer than necessary around my machine, and maybe I flirted with him a little bit—why not, he was so young, so sweet. Ten years later I'm crying in his office, the room smells of big books, and he's looking at me like a father behind his desk.

I might have lost the case if Hagop had come to court. Vosdanig's shirt was wet in the summer heat; I gave him my handkerchief for his face; when it was all over he said:

"One year."

He could have said twenty: I never spoke to Hagop again.

I had told Petrus that I didn't want to see him, that I wanted to be alone for a while. But one afternoon he was standing outside of Barakat's factory, his eyes sunk in his skull, no collar on his shirt. He said he had come to see me smile for it was as good as food.

Stone clouds, no rosy fingers in the sky, only a jaundiced streak on the horizon verifies the dawn; his old fedora tight in the bleak wind, stiff toes steady on the frozen pavement, he walks slowly down to the docks, careful not to fall from weakness. Enough tobacco in the pouch for two cigarettes, one for the ferry across and one for the return: tomorrow stop smoking. In the cafe by the pier he treats himself to eggs, toast, jelly, butter, and cups of coffee, plenty of milk and sugar though he usually likes it black: tomorrow stop eating. Logs bob in the fecund stagnant slime that the ferry slushes and churns around rotten pier poles, smooth, green as if covered with velvet. The first taste of smoke is delicious: he holds the match like a burnt offering and flips it into thick water. He doesn't sketch anymore: he stopped drawing when his hand was stopped by the blank inimical paper, pencil loose in limp fingers, the tender point suspended in void (like his hand dangling in the darkness instead of knocking on her door), he could draw nothing as if his eyes saw nothing, the longer he deliberated the less there was to copy, to study, the illuminations were gone, his imagination empty. His eyes freeze to the river. The ferry docks like a ghost ship that moves without motion. The city waits. A mile through a ghost crowd, sidestepping unhappy faces. Finally he's high above it all, at a bench in a corner, under a metal lamp, his bald head warm under the low light. And as if Time

respects him, as if it is Time itself that has retreated to
out there in the rest of the world, he sits at his leisure,
polishing silver, twisting silver into ancient designs, a
stone here in the eye of a snake, a stone there in the coil
of a snake, mesmeric doodles: he's paid enough for his
room, for sleep, delicious sleep: better to be hungry than
sell apples, than sell his birthright, the right to do nothing, nothing at all: one, two, three, four, ten hours to the
end of day, dusk like an itchy flophouse blanket: the
ferry labors back to the Palisades and he smokes his last
cigarette in tribute to ominous rock. For dinner he'll go
to the *khavah* for olives and bread.

But in the Hunchak Social Democratic Club only
dusty water glasses on the backgammon table. He plays
a few hands of *ouchli* with the proprietor, does not ask for
a cigarette and does not receive one, walks to his room
drunk with hunger, reads in bed, a forty-year-old bachelor with no mirror on the wall. *Even if she loves me, what
am I worth, what could I give her?*

(Last night I took Nembutal for the first time in my
life—and surely not the last. Slept twelve hours! Noises
woke me throughout the night and morning but I went
right back to sleep! Delicious! I got the pills from an old
Japanese doctor in the neighborhood who when I sat
down and told him my troubles looked at me with
oriental indifference and said: "You doh nee sleep.
Sleep is fo people who doh wanna live." But he reached
into his closet and gave me a bag of pills anyway. I usually burn doctors; in England there was no problem,

but in America I owe hundreds of dollars for my teeth, my rash, my rheumatism and my sinus to dentists, doctors, dermatologists, and chiropractors all over the country from New Brunswick to San Geronimo. But I think I'll pay that old Jap: the pills alone would have cost a couple of dollars, but that's not why: he really didn't want to give me pills. Had I taken his advice and walked out I'm sure he wouldn't have charged me, so I'll pay for my own extravagance: after all, he was right. Anyway, I woke up relaxed and pleasant. I even played with the cat though she just scratches her ear and ignores me. I treated her to a few slices of salami with her morning slop and then went outside. The sun was high, the breeze was calm, my knees felt infantile, weak and supple: blessed be science at least for a few moments' peace a pill creates: I walked around the corner to get the paper, slowly, careful to enjoy each step. A girl hitchhiking by the traffic light got my glands going, but for once I was satisfied just looking: she was a delicate flower of China, a veritable delight: Ah, a deep yogic breath and a sigh! I reached into my pocket but lo and behold I had only a nickel and four pennies for the machine. So I asked her if she had a dime for nine cents. She looked long and deep into her purse but *No, sorry, I don't have one,* with a Peking opera smile. *Thank-you* and I turned around to go back. On my way I saw a paper on the steps of a porch so I started to read it; a guy came out of the house and said, "You can have it if you want. We never read it. I just subscribe 'cause my nephew's the newsboy." Bountiful day! The mailman, the milkman, the gas station man, even the policeman is smiling! Ah, America, give me more sleeping pills and I will love you. All's well with the world.

It ended in the middle of cornflakes with the first news item to hit between the eyes, a small sentence of a short war report pushed to the margin by a leviathan cigarette advertisement: "We just fly the worst cases here to American hospitals; next we'll bring a boy of twelve whose face was blown off by a shell.")

We came, my son and I, here to this house where I have been since. We lived downstairs on the first floor then. Mrs. Del Purgatorio knew I was a divorced woman but I was not Italian to bring shame to her house, and I wore black; she said okay, twenty dollars a month, no animals, no men visitors.

I'm thirty years old; in the morning I walk Yero to school— he was a few months too young for kindergarten but I cried in the principal's office and they let him in; all day behind my machine I worry about him, does he eat his lunch, does he drink his milk; after school he goes to his grandmother's who gives him things he likes, tells him his mother is wicked; at dinner he asks once too often then gives it up—"When are we going to have dinner with Papa?" After he's in bed I sit in my kitchen and as if I had not had enough of it during the day I SEW: *clothes for my son, for myself, maybe some mending, doilies, seat covers, useless doodles, anything to fill the night; the house is clean, food is ready for to-morrow, clean sheets on my bed, I have taken my bath, cut my toe-nails, fingernails, I don't know how to read, there is no radio, no phonograph, no telephone—and even if there were? I don't think of Petrus—I know he's there when I'm ready and when I want him. The lamp is warm on my loneliness; there have been nights more painful. Curls in his mustache, chest out like an aristocrat, spats and a cane: what woman does he lie with, to whom does he give what he knows of me, what whore gets paid for my failure?*

One night in Indian summer, Yero asleep upstairs, I carried the garbage outside, dumped it in the barrel by the curb, turned the empty can upside down and sat on it near the stoop by the Chinaman's laundry. The nights were so warm whole families would sleep on the fire escapes. The sun was gone but the orange moon was fat as a pumpkin and there was a light in the air half street-lamp half glow of the sun still lingering, the kind of light I sometimes see in happy dreams, thick colors in soft shapes. That music like the cries of a cat in heat came from the Chinaman's back room and the fishy kerosene smell of his cooking, poor man. I was usually afraid of him, I don't know why, the mole on his nostril and his broken teeth and the sick color of his skin always scared me and in thirty years I never spoke to him but to nod hello past his window as he'd be ironing. But that night even he could have come and sat next to me. Monderstein's candy store was still open across the street and some of the older boys were sitting legs dangling on the newspaper stand: the streets were never empty and I was never afraid to be alone outside at night. I was tired and warm and felt peaceful sitting and watching everything around me, as an old woman might who had nothing to worry about anymore. I watched the trolley come clang–clang up from Paterson Plank Road, like a train I imagined carrying something I had always been waiting for. And then, slowly as it passed, passed my husband's face framed by the moving window. His eyes were blank; I guess mine were too. And in that slow second I felt all the pain of our fourteen years together easily, without any pressure, slip out of me that had for so long been raveled and knotted inside where no joy could ever reach: I watched the back of the trolley which became his back hum lightly away along the electric wires, toward Highpoint Avenue, toward his mother's house, once mine too, and suddenly I was smiling: I felt sorry for him, my son's father, wished he would marry again, be happy as I could never make him happy, and I began to love myself for this feeling—I was free of him, no more burning in my brain.

Where was Petrus? I wanted him now, his soft eyes, his bald benign freckled head, I wanted to make him happy, what difference did it make that he had no money?

Cockroach Oskan came instead. You remember him when he used to visit your father; he was almost a hundred then and he still climbed the stairs. He was not much younger when he moved in with Yero and me. With raisins and nuts in one dusty pocket and stale bread in the other. He was called Cockroach because he slept on the floor, put paper in his shirt to keep warm in winter, tied rubber under slippers and wore them as shoes, never changed his clothes, cut his hair nor took a bath, was one of those men whose body lost all the polish and shine we like to think make us different from animals. The story was—Annah Bahjee had told me who herself had heard it as a little girl in Diarbekir—that he was in love with his brother's wife and came to America, it was said, not to escape the Turks or to find gold but because, like myself, he was an outcast. Whatever the story something had happened to make him different because like a farmer or shepherd who doesn't come down from the hills he didn't live by the fashion of cities. Whatever: it didn't matter to me, to me he was an old man whom the children enjoyed like a shaggy animal, and there was always a part of me that remained child, I never lost the need for an elder to take the place of my father.

He had heard the gossip about me, Melina living alone like a whore. He came one night while Yero and I were at dinner and I asked him to sit down and join us. I scolded him when he took hard dirty bread from his pocket and crumbled it in the barley soup I poured in his plate; I told him I had fresh bread, he could give his crumbs to the birds; but he ignored me, would not waste a morsel, broke it into the soup and slurped it in his sloppy mustache. He came again, then once more, and on the fourth time said he would like to move in, pay half the rent if I would cook for him at night. It would stop the gossip he said and we'd be doing each other a turn. He slept in Yero's room snoring on the floor flat as a corpse with his mouth open and his nose in the air. He was out of the house at dawn quiet as the mice; where he went every day I don't know but he was always back before dinner to play ouchli with Yero. I never saw him wash yet he did not stink: to me he smelled more like the odor of wood or sawdust than the stale sweat of flesh. The three of us were happy together.

It lasted two months. Then I heard of the talk. Zaroohe Sourian told me what was being said in Annah's kitchen: how I was so incontinent even an old man could be my lover. I felt as if there were four walls around my world so high so thick with blame that no penance or recompense could ever scale me free. Oskan said let them talk, they've been talking about him for fifty years and it felt good to be famous. But I couldn't laugh. If I could leave, if I could join another world, I wouldn't need a good name among my husband's people. But where could I find another people out there between West Hoboken and Fresno where everyone lived with only their own kind; where was I to take my son, away from his father's people? I told Oskan he had to move; he said I would trap myself if I went along with their rules. In the back of my mind I knew that I would someday marry Petrus; that disgrace would be enough to bear; I had to conserve something righteous.

(Cockroach Oskan, my hero! Glory be to Cockroach

72

Oskan to give the good name of Hobo to my past! Cockroach Papa, my precedent! May I someday follow in his footsteps, spit in the garden and snort a short buzz of indifference to righteous societies. May I someday have the courage to let go of wanting more and yet more than a hard floor under my head for a bed and stale bread in my pocket for breakfast. May I tell the Welfare Office to shove their determinations up their rumps, and tell the Unemployment Office to go fuck themselves, I don't need no goddamn reason to be "eligible" for "benefits." Someday, somewhere I'm gonna be free of homesickness.)

I loved Petrus. Don't ask me how, how much, why, what for. I was fifteen when I first became a wife and more than twice that when I married your father. For some it takes longer to learn how to love and for others the chance never comes at all. Write luck on my forehead, love found its way in my kismet: from Adana to Beirut to West Hoboken, from the shame of my first period to the fear of a penis to the selfishness of pregnancy: I wouldn't want to go through that journey again without it. But the smile of my fortune was upside down on the man who helped me find my way, may he rest in peace; I had my first husband to thank who suffered through my changes, Hagop whose every breath, step, sniffle, pleasure and pain I learned well enough to understand what MAN *meant and how to cherish and not fear the difference. I loved Petrus after my belly was speckled with stretch-marks and my thighs and my arms and my breasts were soft and loose like fruit ripe enough to enjoy.*

But you can't build happiness on another's anguish. Hagop never remarried. The first night Petrus moved in Yero asked me:

73

"Is uncle going to sleep with you?"

"Don't you want him to?"

"Why doesn't he sleep in my bed and I can sleep with you?"

I didn't know how to answer. I said:

"Because we're married now and married people sleep together."

But it took a long time for my first-born to understand, and sometimes I think the part of Yero that doesn't speak, that part of him I can never reach no matter how much he hurts me or how much I give him, that part buried in his past has never forgiven me.

(It's too late for the harvest, the country's falling apart, and something's rotten in the state of the Union: shit's flying in the wind, froth floats on the water. We live and think within horizons and there's no room left, no way out: the bugs they breed behind barbed wire are waiting, waiting.)

He could not sleep or lose any time lying next to her. He woke at dawn, propped his head with his hand, elbow in the pillow, and stared long and unfulfilled at her profile in the half-light of early morning, the lips, nose, eyes he kissed all night long and could not get enough of nor fix hard enough in his mind, she was too beautiful to know. He let his head sink back into the pillow and shut his eyes to taunt himself a little and then opened them again to see her still there and once more plunged into her warmth, the sweet smell of her hair. Outside the sparrow chirp, the pigeon cuckle, the junkman's horse clippety-clop and the milk bottle clink and the trolley clang, all for him, sang and celebrated his happiness.

There was a tunnel under the river now and the ferry was gone. He rode a bus to work and inside the bus he studied the faces of his happiness and all the women on the bus enjoyed his love and all the men shared his pleasures.

He left work as soon as possible to rush back to her. His boss said, "You better take it easy; you're not young anymore, you know."

On his way home the neighborhood rejoiced.

" 'Lo, 'Lo," the Chinaman waved, with a smile of broken teeth.

(Man is born to be happy or I'll dig up my father's bones and feed them to the dogs.)

When Melina did not conceive no matter how often he tried he began to think he was sterile. She told him she had trouble once before but he couldn't believe her. *Perhaps there is a price to pay for happiness.*

(What is the price of the morning star? How much does the dawn cost? Who gets paid for an egg sunny-side up and the twinkle in the salt? Pay, pay, pay with the stench from my genitals, slime in my mouth, my eyes white with fungus, skull full of maggots, the entire shit and boodle of my cancer, for that one swift spot of time when She loved me, the Old Bitch gone in the teeth, the Ghost in the weed garden. Pay with the entrails of my hysteria, the vomit of my despair, for the Light that made me blind: there is more to day than dawn. Pay on the rack of memory: once She smiled and said, "I want to have children with you," and it seemed that the compost of my father's flesh would finally bear fruit. But She went back to her cave, and I never saw her again.)

And then she's pregnant!
Of the dark past a child is born.
Write a new name on the face of the earth.

(My birth: how did it happen? The National Recovery Act: bridges, tunnels, public buildings, roads, and a war: the Lady is smiling.)

The ancient face in the wicker basket looks twisted and angry. What can he do to make it smile?
Jujube lips, Doo-doo fruit, Hokee-doon, smile, my Hokee-doon, my Home-Hope, Yav-roum, my Yav-roum.

(In the photo from Yero's box camera my father holds me on his lap with his huge hands and I stare suspiciously as if to say no to everything. But his face is plump with happiness.)

Bright snow in the sun; mesmeric crystals freeze all vision. Too much happiness: as if it had been in reserve, frozen forty years, it now rushes upon him in spate.

(While he was riding a Public Service Bus going through the Abraham Lincoln Tunnel under the Henry Hudson River to New York City, on the morning of January 2, 1943, when he was fifty and I was three years old, a blood clot caught my father's brain.

I can only imagine what he was before then.

When I try to understand what his life and death mean to me I see a little man descending from a high plateau, silent, a Buddha smile in a pure face of no one, everyone: a limp hand beckons me to come, come.

My mother tells me not to look. But she's earth-bound, this country or that, no matter, home is where she can cry in her food. I wear her features, I am of her body, and my father offers me nothing, nothing. But there is no choice. His smile is much too benign.)

Before he got sick we would go out wheeling your stroller, and the sun, live on your face, was like our love, free to enjoy.

Write happiness on ice, my amanuensis: it ended one white morning when he kissed us goodbye and closed the door behind him.

In slush two ambulance boys brought back half a man with a hand sunk between his thighs, mouth twisted, and eyes like pebbles in water.

There was no hope: I paid the doctors as if praying to personal gods of a strange religion: they gave him seven years.

Life like love should end by death, not linger and deliquesce like the heaps of sludge at the end of winter, black and crusted. He wanted to surrender: eyes frozen to the ceiling he would not move rather than delay death: a remnant life unfit to endure another season he waited for death and waited until I could endure no more and told him he had at least to go to the toilet alone or I would have to put him away; I bought a cane from the hospital and forced it upon him like a cross he had to carry from room to room, and he suffered you to help him bathe and dress and survive in limbo.

I used to watch the two of you together and think of how a flower withers to become fruit, the end of an apple you always said looked like a dead spider and made me cut away. I could have put him away. At that time of life when I was ready to enjoy him and myself most I would slip in bed beside that side of him dumb to my lust and waited, waited for my change of life. It did not come in time: we don't change when mind decides body has had enough of one season and is ready for another: long before he died I was afraid to stare at other men. You ask about my beauty with diffidence. Do you think your father married this white hair, these false teeth? I was thirty-seven when I had to catch up with him who was suddenly old like fruit cut open and left in the sun, his skin thin and dappled with the stains of age.

Why did I hold on? We did not suffer together because of love; love is no cause, and duty is an empty reason for pain. In the beginning when he learned to use the cane to walk from one end of the house to the other and back again and back, and there was no sign of death to save us, I felt I was being punished for what I had done to Yero and his father: I had to pay for my wantonness. But was it wrong to want a love of my own license? Were the scars on my belly seals of a debt? Did the stretch-marks of my first born, like rain on sand, spell a destiny and sprinkle my flesh like a sacrifice to pay, pay, pay? But for what evil the agony of my life torn asunder to rot in a paralyzed husband? When I searched my past there seemed nothing that was not culpable. Was I born guilty? Further and further back I delved until there was only sand: "Go," my mother said, the soldier's scimitar between her hand and mine, "He will give you something to eat." What had she done to see me severed from her arms? Was my mother the avatar of our first mother's sin? And I? I tell you tales of my childhood in a garden, Melina upon a donkey, calling to her mother: Doo-dee! Doo-dee! *I would repeat them to myself over and over like beads of prayer as if they were proof of my innocence.*

What freedom would I find if I put him in a sanatorium? I felt like water on sand with nowhere to escape. I gave in. And began doing each day what had to be done by going through a motion of poses assumed in repentance. And sent you to church with a nickel in your hand to pray for him. Did you ever light a candle for your mother? You needed her to be strong. And you were my strength, my refuge: when I would slip and lose myself, when I looked up from my sewing or whatever it was that had to be done and suddenly panicked because I could not find myself, I thought of you: my only solace was to watch you grow: you became an extension of myself into a world I could not enjoy: I did not realize I would pay for this too and one day see you sever yourself and leave. Yero was gone already: he scattered his clothes behind for me to wash and iron: it was more than too much that I had taken him from his father, I could not ask him to stay home after dinner: "Where are you going, my son?" "I'm going out. I'll be home late." When I needed someone for talk and you were in your own world of toys under the gas range, who sat across the table? He would nod and frown at my conversation. There were no visitors. Of all his friends not one could bear to see him in that condition, or so they said: rather, I think, they were glad it did not happen to them and stayed away so not to be reminded. I lie in bed facing the window open to the alley; a bit of moonlight falls through the pane; I smell with disgust and pleasure kerosene and incense fumes rising from the Chinaman's kitchen down below; you startle from a dream and crying come to lie on my breasts, for warmth, for someone to hold, and I try to grapple you to myself but you squirm as if to remind me you're my child and you need me to be strong; there is no one, not another to take hold and I, in the middle of my life, cry for my mother.

(Kick him in the shin! Kick the old cripple down! Kiss him: his tears, mucus, wet stubble, spittled lips.

But kick him in the shin until he's sobbing like a child! Kick him! Hate him for his twisted hand and feet of clay!

And kiss him.)

Through the kitchen window the sun slants like Vermeer. Like a Vermeer woman he sits on the *sedir* reading one of my comic books stacked on the radiator cover, his right hand sunk in his crotch.

I don't bring any friends home.

One afternoon I'm sick in school and the nurse wants to walk me home. I tell her I know the way but she doesn't listen. When we reach my street I tell her, "Okay, you can go back now," but she just smiles. When we get to my house I tell her, "You don't have to come up; it's four flights." When we reach the top floor I thank her, "Thank-you very much; goodbye." But she doesn't understand: if she opens the door she will see it, hunched in the corner by the window.

She says to it, "Your son is ill. Will you tell his mother when she comes home from work that Aram was excused from school today?"

A guttural moan.

When she's gone I lie next to him. He smells warm and I fall asleep in his lap.

"Aram, help him off with his clothes."

The arm drops dead when I let it go; the curled fingers don't stay straight when I bend them back. But the hard nails are shiny and smooth hair waves from the elbow to the back of the hand and wiggly veins pulse from the knuckles to the wrist: if the arm is alive why can't it move?

"Aram, stop playing with his arm!"

With his other hand he motions for her not to mind.

"Should I take his shoes off, too, Ma?"

"Yes, but don't play with his foot. It's not a toy."

The right shoe, distorted, keels with the arch up, club to the floor, a perilous boat for my tin soldiers. Across the ocean of linoleum a line is scraped to mark its path from the kitchen to the parlor and back again and back where he walks with his cane.

If I hunch a little forward I can fit the cane in my armpit.

"Aram, walk straight and stop imitating him! Go in the bathroom and see if he wants you to wash his back. I'll be there in a few minutes."

His body is lithe and graceful and beautiful in the luminous water. Tiny beads of bubbles float to the surface from the undulating hair of his chest and loins. Soft folds of skin fill the neck of his fat penis; his big balls sway gently in the current.

He lets me pour water over his head with the silver dish my mother told me he made before I was born.

"How did you make these designs in it, Papa?"

With his good hand he pinches his fingers as if holding a pencil.

Home: *Doon* of intrepid ants and cockroaches, mice in the secret darkness: *Doon* where plastic buffalo roam, under the gas range: where Indians live on the worn-out linoleum plains, near the insecticide powder.

My mother is always washing, cooking, cleaning, sewing, shopping, and asking me to please be a good boy.

Yero is rarely home except to eat and sleep; I'm frightened by him and stay out of his way.

But my father is all mine: I love him.

Asdvats Dada, please make him better!

And my mother never obeys me when I yell at her. I shout at her the names I learned in the streets: *Bum, Dope, Stupid!* She ignores me: I dump toys all over the floor, pull the light plugs out, scream, scream!

"Okay, you're going to bed."

"No! No, you big Jerk, you Crumb!"

And he doesn't change her verdict; unable to defend me he just sits, mouth half open.

And I kick him in the shin.

And I kick him in the shin.

"Shan tzak!"

She rushes to the washing machine for the stick she uses to lift hot laundry from the tub. I climb on the *sedir* behind him and hug his neck; his face is wet with tears.

"Shan tzak, shan tzak!"

I crouch behind him. With his left hand he motions for her to stop.

"Shan tzak!" she shouts—Son of a bitch!

"Tzt," he says with his tongue and his teeth—Don't call him that.

Over the blackboard next to the flag in Fourth Grade, the grisly face of Lincoln, like my father's, stares at me from every angle.

He's going to die. My mother told me he had another stroke and he can't live anymore.

(His bed is the last at the end of the ward. Lysol and urine burn my nose. I sit on his bed and wipe the spittle from his chin and kiss his mouth, his eyes, his smooth soft head.

But there's no response, not even a twisted smile.

"He doesn't smile, Ma."

"Yes he does; look at his eyes."

Small gray eyes, deep in his skull, like Abraham Lincoln's.)

After he was gone and Yero had left for the army, my body began to change and you always complained that I was always crying. One morning I found a yellow spot of starch on your sheet and realized you were changing too.

If I could ask no one else in the world surely my own son could listen to me? could fill with compassion the hollow where a love had slowly died? I was no longer a wife and no longer a woman. And no longer a mother, too? In my change of life I turned to you for pity.

But no son should see his mother change into a sobbing child. When I was young I never forgave Annah Bahjee for being pathetic: she had no right I felt to ask me for pity. I yelled at her just as you yell at me. Poor woman, may she rest in peace, my mother-in-law kept that bathtub distillery not for money but to hold on by bootleg to what she could not expect legally, the honor a mother no longer nor maybe ever could find in place of love. She sold aracq to the young as I bake paklava for them: loneliness is when you have to ask for love. I've earned no pardon from it because I'm a mother. On the contrary I turn from my own to your unhappiness. I once thought I could conquer it with wisdom, as if age could grant a peace that comes with understanding. I have plants on the windowsills now and each morning I tend to them, study them, and try to understand. It seems that with the years I grow more and more stupid.

I could not save my mother: she died behind my back.
Nor can I ask you to stay when you come to visit me.
But I keep your room clean and neat; in your absence I prepare your bed.

Voyages

Each day I expect you to come, until I fall asleep in the silence.

You scold me for always indulgently calling myself an old woman.

I'm only pension age you say and should learn to enjoy my freedom.

Alone and free I worry inordinately over whether or not to get a new kitchen set or keep my old one.

Small things upset me and my daily concern is for the weather.

My bones are cold, my son. Please don't fall down because I won't be able to pick you up.

A wife, a babe, a brother, poverty and a country, which the Greek had I have.

from the journals of Emerson when his first child was born

Born again, goddamn! Every morning the same old story: brain spewing the slimy web: self-pity and hate and where's my lover, when's she gonna come naked to my bed?

Dish din and water crashing in the sink: an old woman's morning ablution, quotidian baptism dawn after dawn: Demeter will live forever and I'm doomed! No more life, Ma, I don't want it anymore!

"There's kebab for your lunch," she says on her way out. "It's good to have you back, my son."

Cataplexy: body sinking: like my father I lie frozen to the ceiling.

And then slowly, in the collage of paint and plaster, a crack in the ceiling becomes the vague face of an angel.

"Hurry," she whispers, "there's no time; you must atone."

"With who?" I whisper back.

"Your little brother."

"I have no little brother."

"There! Look!"

I close my eyes and suddenly I see around the corner

86

a beautiful child in corduroy and flannel sailing popsicle sticks in a gutter puddle.

"O my child!"

But when he looks up and sees me coming he disappears.

Where has he gone? O where is he going?

The door opens and you, Yero, my big brother, walk into your former home and say to me:

"What the fuck you still doin in bed?"

You wear disguised denim, fashion khaki: you're so carefully camouflaged you could be either bourgeois or proletarian. My brother, the American: you've made it: you smell of sweat and cologne.

You've come for the box of photographs on the top shelf in the closet, the stale remnants of our past, pictures of Momma, Annah Bahjee, my father, your father, and the rest of the tribe. I ask you what you want them for and you say:

"I wanna pick out those I like and hang 'em on the wall in my recreation room. Get little frames for 'em and cover the wall."

"Like in a saloon?"

"Yeah, like that. It'll look good, don't you think?"

"Sure, why not? Most of them are dead. They won't be angry."

"What d'you mean *angry?* Why should they be angry?"

"I don't know. I don't know what I'm saying."

"That's for sure. You better get yourself together one of these days."

"How do I do that?"

"I told you a million times but you never listen. Just follow me and you'll be all right."

"Right."

You leave with the box under your arm.

"See you tonight," you say, "I'll pick you up at seven."

I can't explain my sickness to you. You're embarrassed whenever I try to probe the old triangle of my father, your father, and Momma. You fidget with your Zippo lighter and utter inane profundities like *Let the dead bury the dead.* Yet you speak and write their language, dance to their music, marry one of their daughters, send their grandchildren to Armenian Church—you're more Armenian than I could ever try to be. And at the same time more American, not even your old buddy Frank Sinatra could be more American than you in your immense warehouse brain of Hollywood films and make-believe music. Somehow you've managed to make it both ways. Then what is the grief that hides between your temples, my brother, my half-brother, O my dispossessed brother?

I'm tired. It's your turn to say something about your father and grandmother. But no, you never learned how to speak. You'll hang them in your television room and cry in your sleep.

You always call me *Kid,* though I'm more bald than you and with my sideburns and Salvation Army clothes

look more like your uncle than your *kid* brother. We're
in your new Ford: you're a Ford man just as you're a
Lucky Strike man, a man of values and discriminations.
And in my nightmares I hide behind you when the Gestapo stops us and asks for identification: I point to you
and say, "I'm with him, I'm his kid brother, I'm American too." Yes, I'm safe in the close warmth of your car,
down the viaduct to the tunnel, make-believe music
coming out of your ashtray. In the shadows of dusk I
challenge your profile, every inch my mirror, and I
watch you smoke, and as if we are of an exotic Siamese
mixture I feel the smoke in my lungs and out again as I
watch it stream out of your nose. Suddenly you fart.
Farts, burps, the foreign noises of the internal gurgita-
tions of other men once disgusted me. And if they were
intentional, if a stranger announced himself with a short
buzz or yawped for an intimacy I was forced to accept
as if I had to share in his life, then my disgust festered
into hate, hate for the strange life poisoning me through
my ear, like the incessant sinus wheezing of a monster
nose in a theatre or library invading my brain—once in
a dormitory room I almost killed a guy who snored so
violently I put a pillow on his face. It was not the noise
itself: I had nothing against crickets or sewing machines, nor women and the great mystery of their holes,
the soft ululation of a girl snoring on my shoulder; the
small flatus, the humble burp, the deep muted rumble
in her belly, her strangeness was part of desire. But all
men except myself were ugly. And my own noise, the
odor of my own underwear and the stuff like myrrh between my toes were never but delicious. So too when
your fart does not disgust me do I realize how much I

love you, and remember how in my childhood I once believed you and I were the same person separated only by time. I want to stay in the car with you and move and keep moving, my half brother, across the continent, through the night's thick darkness where we see nothing ahead and nothing behind us, and talk long and deep as the moon makes an arc across the sky, and laugh as the dawn light appears and the sun streams out: we'll breakfast in the mountains and rest by an old river, then move on again, westward to sand, north to snow, south to jungles or back here to cities: wherever, the world would be ours, for what could harm two brothers atoned, back to back? My eyes fall, drop suddenly from your cigarette to your hands on the steering wheel: they're the same shape as mine, of the same mold, but they're stronger. I'm afraid of your hands, O my brother, the lithographer, Union man, hands of stone, golf on the weekends, dyed henna color with nicotine: if we ever fought you could finish me in a round, seconds after the bell. How could you ever come with me, leave your wife and kids, the late show and mortgage, prodigious dreams of power lawnmower, snowblower, freezer in the basement to store half an elephant for a future famine, bomb shelter in the backyard, and someday a guided tour of the moon—what could I offer you instead but the sickness in my skull? You light another cigarette like Humphrey Bogart who died of cancer and I ask you how come you smoke Lucky Strike.

"It was the brand I started with and I just stuck with it."

"But why did you first choose it?"

90

"How the fuck should I know? Why do you ask so many stupid questions?"

But don't you remember, my brother? Pearl Harbor bombed on your birthday, twelve years old from the Depression, and in the great family of America patriotic Luckies change colors from green and black to red and white, and you too want to join the insignia of star and circle, wear an AAF T-shirt, collect junk rubber, pledge to Louis Mayer with technicolor allegiance: smoke, my brother, smoke! pray to the Great American with the huge golden leaf in his arms, the tribal manna.

You make a left at Varick Street and drop me off at the pier. I walk a few steps away as you make a U-turn toward Canal Street. Then I realize I forgot to ask you about picking me up after work. I turn and . . . but I can't say your name: I pause, finally whimper, "Hey!" But you're gone.

Never by name, never had I ever been able to call you by name. If you can remember back you will not be able to recall that I ever addressed you; even when I spoke about you to Momma you were always *aghper*— brother. Even now it strains my lips to say *Yero* aloud, *Yerevan, Edward* in English, *Eddie!*

It's about a quarter of an hour before the shape-up. I'm shy when the other guys see me coming. As if they're all your surrogates—indolent, graceful, hard-nosed and sullen, smoking, bullshitting about the ball game—I'm afraid they will reject me, this queer kid walking in like a camel. I hunch to a lonely spot on the pier; lights like jewels glimmer across the river on the Hoboken horizon; thick water laps at my feet. The trucks start coming in. A guy dressed like you, with a porkpie hat and a cigar in his mouth, comes out of the office and blows his whistle. We form a semicircle around his lectern. I want to hide my hands in my pocket: my typewriter hands will betray me. But then, in defense, as if I have to protect myself, instinctively with my old schoolyard style, feet apart and hands loose, belly in and shoulders loose, waiting to be choosed in, I spit a glob and wipe it with my shoe, pawing the ground as I once used to test my sneakers before a game. Yet just one curious disgruntled look from Porkpie and I wither back into diffidence and think *Okay, I'll sit this one out.* He nods to the regulars, grunts:

"Okay, you, you, you, and you. Comon, comon, you wanna woik or pull yer meat?"

After he checks them all in he turns to the rest of us.

Something's the matter with me, my brother, and it wears the wrinkled face of my hand. I stare at the lines in my palm as if I'm doomed.

When I look up, as if coming up for air after just trying to drown myself, I catch his eye, Porkpie with an angry leer: as if he will not pity me, will not let me drown, points at my eyes and nods. I look around and hesitate; he says:

"Comon, comon, you wanna woik or pull yer meat?"

I walk up and he writes me in, and says:

"Join Gang Five and no dickin off."

92

I'm in! Porkpie slips me in where the humanities have failed: I'm going to make some money.

Gang Five is five other guys and I make six: on oranges and grapefruits: two guys inside the trailers swinging the crates down rollers and the rest of us stacking.

Can I say I'm happy? justifying myself in Time with the five other guys at the truck, with all the other trucks at all the other piers in every other city with every other orange and Porkpie and teamster in the world? I'm happy: my muscles quiver to cold fruit, fruit odor and wood odor, not for money though money defines my labor, but because my body tastes of fruit, I can taste my body. After a couple of hours a sweet fatigue flows in my blood, my lips taste of salt, my lungs are clean and cool. After four hours the whistle blows not as a relief but a reward.

I eat cheap imitation hamburgers as if they're a Frenchman's lunch and wash them down with half a giant coke and drink the other half smoking a cigarette, rich toasted tobacco, good for my digestion. I'm by myself sitting by my truck, *my* truck, but I'm not alone: I've made it, I've atoned: I've earned my orange: I pluck it from one of the broken crates: eating it I feel as if the world is mine, I'm one of the guys, and suddenly I feel like reading the *Daily News,* going to the Garden to watch the Knicks, playing the numbers, shooting pool, smoking cigars, blowing half my pay on some broad I'll never see twice: no more museums, no more books, I'm free! I fall asleep on the dolly.

When the whistle blows again I don't have it in me to get up. Four hours' work is enough. But it's my turn inside the truck and the other guys are waiting. The crates now are twice as heavy, and there's something in my neck: a needle sticks inside my collarbone.

"Comon," Porkpie yells, "no dickin off!" He walks by smoking his cigar.

The pain digs deeper. There's another truck and another. More oranges and grapefruits, grapes, cantaloupes, peaches, nectarines, and another needle in my back, one more in my arm, and my legs feel like polio, my lungs like tuberculosis. I can't make it, my brother; I'll never make it. Crates keep rolling, boulders to lift and lower in place for the temples of someone else's religion. The others keep working as if they're slaves. I ask one of them when he thinks we'll be finished and he says he hopes we'll get in a full eight hours. *Help me, Porkpie, please help me!*

"Whatsamatta?" he says.

"I think I'd like to stop now."

"Whattaya mean, *stop?*"

"I can't work anymore; I strained my back."

"Comon, comon, we don't take none a that shit around here."

"No, really."

He looks into my eyes and sees that I mean it.

"Okay," he says, "report to the window and sign out. But don't bother comin back tomorra night."

It's not night, not morning, at three o'clock when all seems too late or too early to start or finish or begin

again: only a stray taxi, a truck, and the intermittent
rumble of the subway footnotes the terrible calm of the
cobbled streets from the pier to your shop. Bums sleep
deep, cuddled pissdamp in garbage: I crouch next to
one and contemplate him snoring through his crusted
nose and mouth: will I ever make it?

In your shop the odor of ink and acid tastes strong
and secure: how did you make it, my brother? What
strength and cowardice made you different from me?
For your sake I offer a politic smile when you introduce
me to the other guys:

"My kid brother: college education and he works on
the docks: ha-ha!"

I wait for you in the office lying on a bench under a
calendar of foam tits and a pink hairless cunt: does She
at least give blowjobs?

I don't begrudge you the money or the trade you've
earned by five years as a messenger boy and five more
as an apprentice, the green years of your life sacrificed
to the Union. But tell me how you held on, what
dreams did you bury between Her legs?

O my brother, you were beautiful once, shaving in
the kitchen sink as I looked up to you from my world
under the gas range: And I worshipped you, a high
wave rolled above your forehead, wingknot in your wide
necktie, fancy plaid shoelaces in your clodhoppers. I
worshipped the Yero of icons, Red Gillette and Green
Jeris and Red-White-and-Blue Burma Shave; delicately
and surreptitiously I played with your model Flying
Tiger and P-T boat; with fear and trembling I adven-
tured through your desk and absorbed all the secrets of
your hands; in your absence I wore your clothes, the

sweaters and shirts that covered me like jellabas, the huge shoes my feet could never fill, the baseball hat not even my ears bent could hold above my eyes: I tried to invest myself with you, you were me in ten years. I studied your photograph album as if it were my future: *Yero in his zoot suit with the Armenians outside the church Easter Sunday; Yero with the neighborhood gang in football, West Hoboken Heroes vs. the Brooklyn Bulldogs; Yero at the Junior Prom like Archie Andrews:* you were never alone: and I would be like you, my hair would wave like yours, my shirt colla would curl, my smile, my stance, my hands in my pockets, my crouch over a football, my arm around a girl, would be yours, in ten years, in ten years I too would belong to the Family.

But I never made it. In the mirror I tried to distort myself, suck in my cheeks, twist my nose, shellac my hair, but it was futile: I was doomed to myself.

And there was nowhere to hide. Sailing popsicle sticks in the gutter puddle around the corner one afternoon I saw you coming up the street, and there was nowhere to hide. I had never seen you in the street before. What does one say to his brother accidentally confronted out there: Hi, brother? Hello, Yero? You kept coming closer, closer.

O my brother, my poor stupid brother! You didn't say anything. I didn't look up. You didn't even stop. I was invisible.

For a long time I did not know how to forgive you. I stayed out of your way when you came home to switch off my Lone Ranger for the Make-Believe Ballroom.

And slowly I began to hate you, the sickness growing inside me as my own body was growing, as I became more and more different from you. When my father died and I didn't need you to take his place anymore you tried to get closer to me, as if he had been the barrier between us. After the burial that cold November morning you took me for a ride in your old jalopy and tried to talk with me, but it was too late. Soon afterwards you were drafted: into the super Family. You made that one, too: platoon, company, and division. You sent pictures from Heidelberg, Stuttgart, Frankfurt, and from your furloughs Venezia, Firenze, Roma: Corporal Yero with mustache and beret on Lido Beach, in an Eisenhower jacket by St. Mark's Cathedral, with the sword of SHAPE.

You came back laughing, cheeks chubby from *Liebfraumilch*. You loved every minute of the army: it connected you to all the idols of your youth from John Wayne to Joe Palooka; it made a *man* of you, proud of yourself and your country; now you could bullshit with as much authority as the next guy; you were *in* for good! You threw away your Hollywood Roll and pegged pants and clodhoppers, the jungle costume of your wild youth, and made the final conformation: Gray Flannel, Button-down, Cordovans, and a pipe after dinner. You lost no time in finding a wife and immediately started getting ready for the Split-level in WASPland.

In all this while you never noticed me until after you got married and moved out, and I never visited you, and you realized that there was something wrong with me, there was something queer about your kid brother: why was he always listening to *classical* music and going

97

to museums? Why did he always want to be *different?*
You said:

"How come you don't read my Zane Grey books instead of all that shit you got there? What's a kid fifteen doing reading Freud?"

And I in all my spite and rebellion told you your books were for stupid people. Your wife, seeing how hurt you were, told me to apologize. When I didn't you lit another cigarette and said to me politely:

"Let me tell you something, you little shitinthepants: the trouble with you is you don't know how to be stupid."

We ride back, this time up Riverside Drive to the Bridge, and over to your house near Paterson. The warm silence of dawn wraps us together: I love to be with you when you're quiet, and I imagine deep thoughts behind your eyes. I'm happy with you in the beautiful flight of the Bridge: without words you have been and will be my brother forever and ever. But I break it with a question; forgive me, my brother, I must hear you speak; out of nowhere I ask you:

"What was your father like?"

"What?"

"What kind of man was your father?"

"What kind of stupid question is that?"

"What did he talk about, how did he feel about things, what things did he like?"

"He liked hot dogs."

"Hot dogs?"

"There was a kosher restaurant across the street

from where he worked. He used to like their hot dogs."

"Only hot dogs?"

"No, he liked plenty of mustard and sauerkraut, too."

I sleep in your guest room. So clean and neat. And quiet! No people making noise next door, upstairs, or downstairs. When your kids get up your wife will politely tell them to go outside to play because Daddy and Uncle are sleeping: outside with the robin and squirrel, no snakes in the thick grass it took you five years to groom, no weeds in your wife's neat clean flower garden: *Play neatly, children, keep the sand in the sandbox.* Your children will be well bred, I'm sure: spic and span little soldiers at attention, who will one day wonder: *What went wrong with Uncle Aram, why does he carry stale bread in one dusty pocket, nuts and raisins in the other?*

Ah, it would be so comfortable if I could stop my mind and enjoy the amenities of your home, the compensations of your sacrifice: sharp hot shower in a warm bathroom, cupboard full of potato chips and assorted cookies, jelly beans and chocolate in the Lazy Susan, and your wife doing everything in her power to please me as long as I'm polite: in this inflated meanwhile of your content, in the lull of pillage and war, before the mad hordes come trampling your wife's tulips. Just think, Yero, you're Che Guevara's age and all he has is jungle rot and asthma.

Forgive me, I get carried away. It's not your fault, the DDT in the tuna fish, the machine laughter in the television, and your father dead leaving only hot dogs to bequeath. You never learned how to speak to yourself and I can't blame you for your dumb silence. But you were my big brother, Yero, and I expected you to stay beautiful. Poor Yero, what has She done to you? You were so beautiful, strong, and intelligent ten thousand years ago, stonecutter on the high plateau, killer of lions. Give Her up, Yero! Let Her go! For your father's sake, your children's sake, for my sake, and your own life, pull out from Her Cunt. I beg you, my brother, O my half brother, my dispossessed brother, don't drip your life away with Her Disease. You told me yourself once when I was nineteen, hitchhiking up to Boston and back for a girl with apple blossoms in her hair: I was at Momma's house packing my bag and you came over to drive me to the freeway: I told Momma I'd be away for the weekend and she didn't ask anything more, but in the car you asked me why I was running around like my balls were on fire: when I told you you said:

"Shit, Aram, if you gotta go more than ten miles to get laid, it ain't worth it."

And you know something, Yero? I never even fucked her: we used to sleep together with our clothes on.

I wandered through my brother's house and tried to come to some kind of peace with his life. In the low hum of the refrigerator I sat in his wife's kitchen while they were all asleep upstairs and tried to figure out how we could all live together without the burning in my head. The immaculate design of stainless steel and white formica hurt my eyes. In the living room and dining room the pastel-blue wall-to-wall carpeting and the shiny heavy drapes and the blank walls and display furniture all together in perfect magazine composition scared me, made me feel sick. My eyes searched for some kind of confusion to break the order, but everything, even the ashtrays, lay clean and in place. Where were the rich colors of intricate rugs and dancing curls of ivory worked in wood, a couple of crazy pillows here and there, some junk and knickknacks scattered around, a medley of different shapes and colors so that the eye could move around and around: his house seemed to renounce the sinuous design of his father's people: all the lines were bent straight and hard.

Very well then, I thought, my brother's modern, up with the times, letting go of the past, and getting his kids ready for the space age.

But that's not what the pictures said, hanging in his

recreation room: brown photographs of Hagop and Petrus, Annah Bahjee, and other dead: picnics at Lake Hopatcong and Coney Island, feasts on the holidays, tambourines, long black mustaches, narghiles, ornate, opulent: eyes askance: faces of the dead in his television room. He did not let them go: he held on, almost desperately, to what I had envied and never known: feasts of marrow bone and garlic, mothers and aunts in the old woodstove kitchen, everyone together: moments he tried to recapture at Thanksgiving and Christmas and Easter and birthdays and anniversaries and any occasion for calling the family together.

What family?

He would tell his wife: "Aram doesn't care, he doesn't care about the family."

But they were my dead, too. That guy there, whom he called *Papa*, with spats and a cane, curls in his mustache, was my first cousin. And that old lady, his grandmother, wrinkled and weary, was my aunt. And that other guy, that bald guy holding him piggyback on his shoulders, wearing a funny woolen top and bottom bathing suit, he was my . . .

Father.

Papa.

Dear Petrus in heaven, what am I going to do about Yero, what am I going to do about my brother, your godson? We share a past together and have nothing to do with one another now. Look down there in the basement, all his tools neatly arranged above his work table: his backyard out there, clean crew-cut grass: and all the warmth and security of this house: I can't feel at home here, and yet we were born from the same womb.

For a long time, ever since I felt different from him, I wanted to tell him what was wrong with his life. I spent years trying to figure out the winning argument, searching for enough ammunition to blow up his life and replace it with what I thought it should be, what I wanted to be. . . .

What?

Hooky days from high school, hopping the red-and-tan bus by the tunnel, I used to go to the city looking for excitement, and with all the blaze of adolescence, walking from the Port Authority to the library and up Fifth Avenue toward the museum, splitting the mobs on the sidewalk with all my anger and spite, hatred for what my own brother was part of, I tried to find someone, something, Saks, Rockefeller Center, St. Patrick's Cathedral, anything or anyone that I could curse and spit upon as if to say: Fuck you and your cordovans and button-downs, I don't give a shit about your world, I know a better world. . . .

Where?

In the museum between the Chinese and Indians and Europeans I searched for answers somewhere in the Near East, between Afghanistan and Egypt, in the cool glimmer of jewels and gold, in the calm spread of a magic carpet.

More, I whispered. I want more . . . of something. Beauty. Something to make me feel good. Because I'm not happy, my brother. I want something more than what you have. It's ugly where you live. It's wrong.

But he could not understand. With a can of beer in

one hand, cigarette in the other, shoes off and empty-faced in front of the television, tired after a hard day's work painting the garage—white—and raking the leaves and yelling at the kids, he seemed to tell me, between burps and farts, his belly full of a big dinner: "Who're you to blow up my life? I'm happy." It was clear to him that he had to be on the right road because so many others were on it: not only with him but before him stretching back even to the high plateau where we came from. There were side paths maybe, going off into the woods or up the mountains. But the main road had to be the one he was on, with the mob, the rabble, the slobs, yes, he seemed to say, I'm stupid and glad of it because I'm not lonely even if I don't got no culture, I got a television and all the other poisons and I like them and I don't care about all the damage or all the suffering out there, so just leave me alone.

So I tried to leave him alone. I went to college and tried to forget about him and the world outside my books and aspirations. About him and all those like him. Thinking we could be brothers and have nothing to say to each other.

And he would tell his wife, as the two of them sat alone at night, with the television off and the kids asleep, she sitting by the lamp knitting, he in his leather chair with the television guide in his lap, in those moments when he would allow himself a little sadness: "I can't talk to Aram. I can't talk to my own brother."

Brother. What did it mean when we said it: brother?

When he was about fifteen he used to be a soda jerk after school in the ice-cream parlor by the park. Those were the days when there were only three flavors and my favorite was strawberry. One afternoon somehow I managed to get enough money for a cone. I went inside and there he was, this guy who was my brother.

"What do you want?" he said, very businesslike.

I was about five years old then and was just beginning to learn how to deal with such important matters. I said, very businesslike:

"I want one strawberry cone, single dip." I did not say please.

And he gave me one strawberry cone, single dip.

And I gave him my money.

And he put it in the cash register.

And I walked out.

Probably that night we ate dinner together at the same table.

That's what brother meant sometimes when I couldn't figure out anything else.

Or it was the silence between us the way animals know their own kind without fear or suspicion.

Silence: it was our strongest bond. That November morning after the burial when all the others went home with the priest he took me for a ride in his new car, that old '36 Ford jalopy he had to start with a crank in the front because it was so cold while I sat all bundled up like a young prince watching him through the windshield huff and puff, blow his fingers and try again, until he finally turned it over. We went up 9W over the Palisades past Nyack to Bear Mountain. It was the end of autumn and all the colors had faded to brown, the river was gray with the winter sky, and there was no heat in the car, but deep in my lungs I was very excited. I had never been up this far before and he let me look out the window long and full not saying anything except to answer my questions. It was a big treat: I could ask him anything I wanted and he would not get impatient. I knew it had something to do with my father just dying but that was all right. I was very big on geography in those days and he answered my questions one right after the other: Yeah, that's the same Hudson River . . . that's right it goes all the way up to Canada . . . no, we're not in New Jersey anymore, this is New York . . . and so forth and so on. Then I could see he was getting tired so I stopped and went off by myself into the panorama looking down, down to the river still winding beneath us. I knew he had wanted to say something about taking my father's place. He was a man now, out of school, working, and had his own car: he would take responsibility for me, he wanted to say.

I was relieved that he didn't. I didn't need him anymore to take my father's place.

When we got to Bear Mountain he bought a hot chocolate for me and a coffee for himself. I felt very proud to sit with him at the counter. In silence. That he didn't talk to me sometimes made me feel that he respected me: that what he wanted to say was too deep inside him: that I would understand without the words.

It was the easiest way: for both of us: it covered over our differences: silence could veil our difference.

Brother: it meant knowing the differences and being able to deal with them.

And then judge?

Did I have to judge my own brother?

His life: born in the back bedroom, September 19, 1929: everyone adoring him in his wicker basket. . . .

Poverty brought everyone together: his babyhood was full of cousins, no radio or phonograph but much music, no meat but lots of bulghur, everything was perfect as far as he could see. . . .

Until he saw hatred between his parents. . . .

And then poor Buster Brown in short pants and a salad-bowl haircut, not yet in kindergarten, taken out of paradise by a sad mother. . . .

He hid his hands in his pockets and shuffled off to school: his beautiful hands that could draw like a whip: scenes populated with Indians and settlers, wigwams and cabins, Eskimos and igloos, wish-fulfilled fantasies of tribes in harmony. . . .

(Our mother saved a few of them, and I cried when I saw the ancient wonder of his innocence, the thick crayon fading from the dessicating pulp, the irreplaceable loss of his talent). . . .

He drew for his own dreams, not for attention. . . .

Because he would be ordinary, unnoticed. . . .

Lost in the middle. . . .

As if to say: Leave me alone, I don't want to stand out, I take no part in the outside. . . .

No part in the war between parents, the strife between right and left. . . .

So that with one foot in his mother's house and the other in his father's he sought a bigger, stronger, more established home. . . .

In the arms of Miss Liberty and Papa Democracy, the Police Athletic League, and the Armenian General Athletic Union, the United States Army, and the Lithographer's Union. . . .

With all the others of his generation with their own

special homes broken in their own special ways, who
sought refuge in Yankee Stadium and the Paramount,
in the corner saloon and Times Square, following Frank
Sinatra and General MacArthur, with Columbia songs
and MGM dreams, with that uniform standard unprovoc-
ative easy mindless credo of Leave-me-alone-I-don't-
want-no-trouble. . . .

There would be no trouble as long as he obeyed the
rules, paid his dues, and pledged allegiance. . . .

To renounce what was already lost, and trade in his
father's hookah for Lucky Strikes, roll up his grandmother's rug and cover his floors with foam. . . .

As if he could eat his shish kebab with ketchup.

And I saw him year by year lose the luster not only
of his father's past but his own personal talent, his beautiful hands become stiff and awkward, bent to golf clubs
and a lawnmower, his wonderful eyes dulled by television and the mindless stone labor night after night ser-
vile to advertisements, his imagination once capable of
cartoon sagas he drew for his own entertainment not
just dulled or rigidified but smothered, suffocated, that
fantastic imagination buried deep behind his eyes where
it could never again see more than the day of his retire-
ment or the last payment of his mortgage.

All that I did not have to judge. It was done. Let the
dead bury—as he said—the dead.

But something, someone had to be judged.

And what he served and let rule not only his own
life but his children's I would have judged and condemned. . . .

As if I knew what to replace it with. . . .

The home he gave his children who I took to the zoo

once a year and awkwardly kissed with displaced uncle-love and sent them music and pictures for their birthdays, the values he gave his children who I ran away from rather than embarrass in front of their peers with my shaggy hair and ragged clothes, the love he gave his children who I could not love half as much, all that I would have judged as if to say: You're wrong, you're bringing them up wrong.

And he would have said to me: Why don't you stick around more and see what you can do?

One night we happened to watch the six o'clock news together. The World's Fair in Long Island had just opened up that day and the screen was full of people who had gone there to protest.

"Protest what?" he asked. "What the fuck are they complaining about?" He wasn't really asking me but I answered him anyway.

"The fair was built for business," I said, "not for the people."

"Everything is for business," he said, "so what? What's good for business is good for us."

And I couldn't answer him anymore. Because it would have meant arguing and arguing meant turning the screw inside his head that would shut off his ears. Because what he really meant was: THE WORLD'S FAIR? The World's Fair was one of the happiest days of my life: trylon and sphere and everyone together when Petrus took me there in 1939: how could they protest my memory: they want to tear my life apart!

Nor could I plead with protesters, my friends, when

they would come to tear his life apart: I could not say: leave my brother alone, he's innocent, he meant no harm. The knowledge of his life, of all the causes and effects that led him to his patriotism and servitude, was useless in trying to help him.

He was confused and distraught and I felt sorry for him.

And then angry again at his relief when the news switched to something more comfortably remote like trouble in South America.

I once sat in a diner with him in Piscataway down south on our way to my college, a small town where no one ever heard of an Armenian before much less saw one in the flesh, and there he was, my brother, bullshitting with the guy next to him and the lady behind the counter about baseball as if he were one of them and they all shared something together, shared his memory of the World's Fair and Tom Mix and Betty Grable all together, and I saw how truly happy he was not to be alone, to know that he could go anywhere from Piscataway to Walla Walla and bullshit with any guy next to him and any lady behind any counter who shared his memory of the World's Fair and Pearl Harbor and Nagasaki.

I walked outside. I could not come to any peace with his life inside the house. It was almost dawn and I wanted some coffee in a diner with big chocolate-covered custard-filled doughnuts on an old stained marble counter.

Try again: my brother lived in the suburbs: I almost forgot: miles and miles of crew-cut grass, five miles to the nearest shopping mall, twenty to chocolate-covered doughnuts at four in the morning.

I went down by the lake and smoked cigarettes. It wasn't far from his house to beautiful water and trees: his children had at least that advantage: a city boy myself, I never did learn the names of birds and plants and sometimes even thought of them almost as a foreign language. It was quiet by the water, peaceful, and the mist began to rise to the soft light of dawn.

I could sit there as long as I wanted: my brother was a citizen of that town: that was what he paid taxes for.

But was it worth it: the dull environment, street after street of nothing, no garbage, no trolley tracks, but nothing else either: everyone together smothered in sleep: no trucks or busses to wake them up, but no roosters either? They would wake up to advertisements on the clock-radio. Give it up, Yero! I wanted to tell him, tear it out and throw it away, it's all phony, false, a trick of discounts, bargains, and installment plans: and the illusion of family, the World's Fair, the stadium crowds, F.D.R.'s fireside chats, were all lies, choke-weeds you must pull out now, tear from your past like you rip thick choke-grass deep in the soil pulling hard, gripping between your legs, tear them out and burn them.

For what? he would have said to me: *To become like you? Do you want me to become like you, Aram?*

The history of my dreams began with the Monster that would climb my infant home, squeeze through the window, and stab Its teeth in my eyes. My bed was next

111

to the alley window, the hollow eyes of chimney pots staring across the roofs in the moonglow like the cowls of Ku Klux Klan, and down below in the cellar, underneath the boiler in the black of grease and oil with the cockroaches and rats, my Monster waited until all the lights were out. It feared nothing. With Nazis, Japs, Communists, Frankenstein, and the Mummy, It would choke me with slime, bite my eyes, and slice my penis: I was the chosen one, the warm sweet blood of sacrifice.

Yet I always survived: out the kitchen window, down the fire escape, through everyone's backyard and into the streets and secret hide-go-seek crevices, doorways, bushes, sanctuaries discovered and held tight in the catacombs of memory, I always escaped, running, lungs relieved suddenly in the streets, MY streets. . . .

No more.

Not even among the sidewalk populace could I find refuge as the Monster began wearing the masks of Police and Government.

All the years of living undercover caught up with me. Comic books stolen from Monderstein's candystore, tomatoes splattered over the Principal's home on Halloween, all the stolen tuna fish, cigarettes, razor blades, all the questionnaires, documents, forms, oaths, and pledges forged and falsely informed, my disguise for scholarship boards whispering "Now here's a promising young lad . . . ," all the buried hatred for teachers, coaches, administrators and officials and my betrayal of their confidence, the counterfeit of good citizenship, and every smile I ever wore to hide my fear, all came back for payment, and I was up for trial, with no haircut and tie, pride or dignity for defense: proud of nothing that was myself in the accidental nation of my birth, I learned never to trust it again after the patriot posters I drew with passionate allegiance, flags and symbols I worshipped hand on heart, and songs I memorized like prayers were used not for my own honor and dignity but for some perverse concoction of money and power in the sick wards of public men.

Chameleon-like, I lived outside my dreams wearing clothes of someone else's inhibitions, obeying mores of someone else's property, passing tests, paying taxes, cheating tests and taxes, surviving in the streeets with camera-smiles and whispering my hatred to window-panes, deep muted hatred for the scrofulous pock-pitted specter of the Law . . . until the Monster gained ground, until It was always there behind my shoulder, waiting for the darkness.

Was I to blame for my own dreams; did I create my own Monster? No voice answered my furious wandering. Only the land, endless, horizon ahead of my fear, extended till I could run no further and stopped at a crossroad in the middle of nowhere, pointed my thumb over my shoulder and hitchhiked backwards, blind to any destination. The land: who owned it? It was mine as long as I kept moving. But if I stopped for a piss, a little rest, or something to eat, then I had to show credentials and pay money for privileges inside hallucinatory neons where fellow citizens stared like characters in a nightmare.

I had to leave. Not for adventure, not for horizons to sing from open freight cars full of hobo-joy riding high and easy quaquaversal over my country, my country no more, no not for adventure this time, but escape: Persona Non Grata stamped in the eyes of my identification, subversive to my own rotten maggot-infested love Pro Patria, I had to find another refuge.

But where, what virgin space would provide asylum? No woodsman, afraid of snakes and the lurking dangers of a dark forest, I could never make it on my own always looking back over my shoulder for the hairy arm of my abominable monster. Where was I to go all by myself on a desolate beach of evil seaweed and bloated creatures sucking bubbles, a sudden tide and the angry crash of green foam, my shoes wet, losing balance on slimy rock, falling! Please, help me! A flock of wild birds electric bright dip and dive in a black wind, then horribly fall and transform to paper in my hands, schizophrenic pieces ripped and scattered into the anguish of my lap. Please help me, someone, please— No, don't come too close, you're ugly. Strangers laugh at me. And what is your name? they ask. My name is . . . my name is. . . . Don't cry, they say, we'll help you, here let's look in the phonebook, and they hand me a giant Bible written with computer dots I don't know how to read. It says here your car's not registered, that's five years in the penitentiary. No, no, my name is . . . my name is . . . here on my driver's license . . . no, that's not my name either, but if you go to the county records in . . . you'll find my life born on . . . on . . . my my mother's name is . . . my father's name is . . . please help me, please.

I would go to England. A friend of mine could get me a job over there: another country over the ocean.

To save money for the trip I worked as a laborer out of the union hall in Newark, shaping up in the morning and being sent out to lay pipe and clear ground for new developments in south Jersey.

That summer I saw my brother on the weekends, taking my mother out of the heat and humidity for barbecues at his place in what she called *the country.*

Before dinner Yero and I drank gin and tonic and watched afternoon movies outside in the shade of his patio. Or I might help him with one of his projects like constructing a swing for the kids by tying a rope from one of the tall trees and hanging an old tire on the end of it. Or building a small house in the branches of another tree, and I tried to match him nail by nail, but he was always much stronger and I could never keep up. And then we washed and drank gin and tonics or highballs with a *mezeh* of smooth rice-and-onion-filled grape leaves in olive oil. Then we made the fire for the barbecue.

Melina was happy to see her two sons together. At dinner she helped his wife, Isabel, fill our plates with heaps of pilaf, shish kebab, juicy charcoal-broiled fat Jersey tomatoes and bell peppers, and we ate all of it, pleasurably like sheiks or pashas, drinking Budweiser beer between mouthfuls, wiping our plates with thin hollow wafers of Syrian bread. And then, stuffed and lazy, we sat back and waited for dessert while the kids played with their friends across the yard zipping frisbees over the wide lawns in the warm air of the cicada buzzing long and indolently. Isabel brought out the paklava or the fruit salad or an American dessert she had made from a recipe in one of her magazines, and Melina served the Turkish coffee which we drank afterwards, smoking cigars, watching the sun go down, puffing slow smoke in the cool breeze of a red sky: the good life: we ate enough that summer to feed a village.

Melina sat under the oak tree by the garden and watched her grandchildren with pride. I made a camera of my hands and spying at her with my right eyeball circled by thumb and index finger I snapped a picture of the old woman enjoying the success of her first-born. She had come a long way from eating orange peels in the gutters of Antioch. They said little to each other, Yero letting Isabel carry most of the conversations with his mother, and then the kids knowing where they could freeload affection took up the rest of Grandma's time. But Yero treated Melina with all the respect due to her according to tradition. He even loved her, but love was an emotion he had trouble expressing outside of family dinners. After sundown they all watched television together and I went to New York to look for some action, driving over the bridge and down Riverside Drive to the Village. Later on Yero drove his mother home or she might stay for the night and Isabel would take her in the morning. With or without me that's how things went for many years, but Melina was only truly happy when her two sons were together. The Family Unit had to stick together, and she could not understand why I wanted to disrupt it. But she became used to my wandering and when the time came for me to leave for England she did not cry.

The Family Unit and the Great White Father guarding us through the television: our own fathers' bones buried across the street from a parking lot, their elements floating in the foam-covered polluted waters of the bay. Both Melina and her older son tried to hold on to whatever tradition remained and kissed each other formally on the cheek when they said so-long until the next weekend. But the unit was weak, crippled like a paralytic with a blood clot in his brain, and one day Yero too would see his children move not just twenty but many many miles away.

What should I wear? I always had trouble packing for my travels. Inevitably I'd take too much, too much underwear, too many socks, or a white shirt and dressy pants I'd never wear. What should I wear in case I met a beautiful woman: would or would she not like me if I looked American?

Corduroy was always safe: neither this nor that; in Sweet-Orr and Huskies I could be mistaken for anyone.

Yero said:

"You can get some nice Harris Tweeds in England."

"I'll send you some," I said.

He said:

"Get them for yourself, stupid. You're the one who needs them, not me."

And so I left. It was the end of summer, cool winds from Canada introducing the autumn. I'd miss the changing of the leaves. But September always did seem the right time to start anew.

High pressure and a beautiful sky on the day I left: New York shining on the horizon: and beyond it, across

Brooklyn, vast spaces of the last view of America, ugliness and all.

The airport was always an exciting place. Poised on the tip of Long Island it seemed entire of itself. It made me feel special, as if, because I was a bona fide traveler with passport and ticket, I could mingle with the international elite and rise above the mass of commonfolk on the mainland.

Saarinen's TWA Terminal with its wide wings made my heart stop as when watching a long-legged bird about to take off. Or like the eagle of E Pluribus Unum. Free and audacious, yawning, arms out, fists hard, with a barbaric yawp over my head. Money made it, I realized, and for a moment paused and reconsidered: maybe things weren't as bad as I made them out to be. . . .

But there was no turning back: suddenly I was on my own, northeast to Reykjavík in the roar of turboprops, one hundred and eighty dollars to the Old World via Iceland: Goodbye, my failure.

This was the last time, I thought. No more running: I would find something, someone over there. I'd be an exile, an emigrant-immigrant—a pilgrim!

Rrrrrrrrrrrrrrrrrrrrrrrrrrrrrrrrrrrrrrrrrrrrrrrrrrrrrrrrrrrrrrrrrrrrrr: for twenty-four hours.

And all the way I stare at the face, tits, ass, and legs of a young Icelandic maiden who should know by my bald head, hooked nose, big black mustache that I'm the ithyphallic Turk who will shove his nose up her cunt and lick her like a beast lapping water: rape her, a satyr whispers in my ear. I will become a new man, leaving my old self behind. And what could she know of the boy crying in the mirror, ashamed of his penis.

She tucks in my blanket thinking I'm asleep. And sleep finally does claim the pleasure I did not have the courage to enjoy.

It was all right about my mother. Yero was back there. Though I could always fly back if she needed me I felt relieved that he was somewhere near her. But too bad he couldn't come, too. He loved being in Europe when he was there in the Army.

We could hit the pubs together, eh Yero?

But he had to stay behind. That was his home back there.

Goodbye, my brother. Goodbye.

And in front of me the very immediate green of Scotland.

We glide sideways into it, descend dreamlike to patches of farms and meadows deep green and brown, reddish brown: new territory.

And we land.

"How much money do you have?" asks Her Majesty's immigrant official.

But it's all right, I expected it: too many freeloaders coming in, Black Jamaicans, Brown Pakistani, Bald Armenians, Beatnik Americans. I'm prepared: money in the bank and promise of employment.

"Have you anything to declare?" asks the customs

man, speaking my language, MY LANGUAGE no more, for now it's with the spruce tongue of his rosy-faced green-eyed dialect.

Smile, Mister, I'm not going to hurt you, I'm looking for a home here; your people once did the same where I came from.

A lorry driver, unable to understand anything I say unless I repeat it twice as if I learned my English in Baluchistan, picks me up outside of Glasgow and gives me a ride due east to Edinburgh, pronounced *Edn-burra*. On our way he stops at a backroom cafe of a petrol station and shows me off to his mates, like John Rolfe returning with Powhatan's daughter. He orders tea for himself and instant coffee for the *Yank*.

"You Yanks like coffee, I know. Here."

"Thanks."

And so the Yank, traveling unsuccessfully incognito in corduroy and washable synthetics, khaki duffel on his hump with an excess of underwear and a plastic bag of his mother's *choreg* (Chrissake, Ma, I can't eat all that— Take it, you'll eat it), made his way on the Grand Tour, expatriated by his own fear and hatred, down the green coast of the North Sea, munching *choreg* over hills of heather, through cobbled streets of little red villages, women ticket collectors, shopkeepers, costermongers calling him *Love, Duck, Darling, Dearie,* all the way to Doncaster and farther to London, the world calling to him with newness, a clean wind reminding him to breathe. . . .

Shakespeare's country!

Oh, it felt good.

It felt good.

It felt good to be away, to see new people, another way of life, good bread, good beer, good cheese, in warm carpeted pubs, small friendly shops, milk in pint bottles, things scaled to my size, as once in America a long time ago maybe, and no monster at my back, or so I thought. . . .

In London, in what is called the *East End* which is itself a large colorful variegated section of the city and perhaps the most interesting—with a reputation sort of like Brooklyn's only it is historically, culturally, and esthetically richer than Brooklyn and more like downtown Manhattan around Mulberry and Delancey—between Whitechapel and Bethnal Green, concealed within twisted streets, hides a small neighborhood that Jack London when he visited there nicknamed *Itchy-Fields*. Its proper name is Spitalfields, from Spital (spi•tăl) 1634 (Late respelling of SPITTLE after HOSPITAL) a foul or loathsome place or. a shelter for travelers. How or why it originally got the name I didn't know, but it proved to be very fitting after the second world war. In the early eighteenth century when the Huguenots first settled there it must have been very attractive. The great Hawksmoor's Christ Church was built there in 1740 and the homes surrounding it, which still stand, were done by his studio in the lovely Queen Anne style of that period.

I did not know all this when I first moved to one of these houses behind the church three doors down from the Rector's. It had become a slum and I found it because it was cheap. The church was in ruins and there was a movement to procure money for restoration or it would be torn down. A huge spiked monolith of Anglican anguish, it towered above everything in the area and there were few buildings in London to equal its massive intimidating beauty. Even black with two centuries of industrial dirt, its two small windows in the front smashed and gaping like the plucked eyes of a martyr, and fenced in by barbed wire, it still commanded your gaze upwards, towards what thousands and thousands of people, with passion and hunger and fear and anguish, once believed in all their lives.

The Great Synagogue was just down the street, and between these two houses of God most of the residences had been taken up by embroidery factories, furriers, tailors, and garment dealers. Around the corner on Brick Lane the Jamaicans and Pakistani had moved in and between the two Pakistani curry cafes late at night you could find a prostitute who would do the business for half a quid or even less. The old meth-drinkers and former whores lay in the grass next to the church much like their cousins in the Bowery. Across the street from the church the entire block was taken up by the produce market, always busy with trucks from dawn till about noon when some of the bums could find brussel sprouts and turnips for free—I found some myself sometimes. Late in the afternoon the odor of rotten vegetables was very pungent and often unpleasant, especially in warm weather or after a rain.

Sometimes the odor and the bums, the empty church and the dark and silent market stalls depressed me, and coming home at night I walked as fast as I could.

But usually I was happy to live there, much rather there than up in Hampstead or Kensington with other Americans and bohemians and pretty girls. I went up there to visit or to go to the cinema, but Spitalfields was my home, and I did not mind the toilet outside in the cold or having to use the public baths around the corner. I thought of my father when he first came to America and sometimes I felt that I was recapturing the flavor of those days I heard about, of nickel beer and free sandwiches, cobbled streets smelling of horse manure. And the church was more often beautiful than not: it was reassuring and uplifting to have a great work of art a hundred feet from my doorstep.

I made friends with the other people in the house, art students and general good people like those you find all over the world, searching and trying new ways of living, and I shared with them going to the flea market on Sunday mornings, eating kippers and smoked salmon, cream cheese and bagels for breakfast back at the house, getting drunk at the pub on the corner listening to Irish music, sitting around the paraffin heater, trading dreams.

And my job was not difficult, teaching at a school in Shepherd's Bush a few days a week, learning, making mistakes, getting outside of myself.

And there was Lofty, down in the basement, like Cockroach Oskan, a big old man with a shock of white hair like a prophet's, his teeth like rotten corn, no socks, his tufted chest bare to the cold, clothes like rags to blanket a horse, good old Lofty, odd-job man, who entertained me for tea and cigarettes telling me stories of the old days, avoiding the war and the shell shock and the five years in the mental hospital, who could have taught me what it's like to be sixty-two years old, no money, no home, no family, and glad to be alive.

And so in the first few months I was happy with so many new things and places and people and came home at night tired enough to fall asleep and sleep soundly.

Then it started again. Dreams of water and birds. The monster reappearing in the streets of London.

Yero wrote back, answering one of my cards:

"Don't worry about not making it home for Christmas, you missed the last forty so one more won't make any difference. We're fine here and hope you have a nice holiday over there."

Places became too familiar, the museums and galleries too serious, and there were no new films left. The streets became heavy and slow, and friends couldn't be asked to relieve loneliness. Enjoy yourself, I kept trying to tell myself, participate with the sky, feel the wind smack in your face like the full splurge of a child's slap upon water!

But like in the museum, the dark past seemed to crouch with monsters, in marmoreal halls of a long history afraid of the night. Something was crippled inside me like the Elgin Marbles, broken and silent in a vacuous chamber without windows: Dionysus had only half a face, and no feet and no hands.

I walked the afternoons away in Soho. Bored with

the strumpets and bookstores I waited for the pubs to open, bullshitted with friends over a couple of pints of best bitter, and went to *Jimmy's,* the Greek restaurant in the basement off Frith Street for lamb stew, salad, and *fasulyah* in the corner, reading the *Evening Standard* smut with Turkish coffee and paklava for dessert.

More beer at night and peanuts, salty vinegared fish and chips walking home drunk, through the soft glow of fog in the amber streetlamps, belly content, praying to Hypnos for sleep, deep and quick, past the whirr of embroidery machines all night long.

And deep in the night cried out beyond the edge of dreams:

"I want a home, some kind of stability, a wife and baby, a different kind of life. . . ."

Like my brother's?

"You're getting old, you should stop fooling around and settle down somewhere," his voice said over my shoulder.

In the mornings I pissed in the sink when I didn't feel like using the john outside. Over my porridge I thought of him eating breakfast with his family. When my laundry piled up I thought of Isabel and her super automatic washer-dryer.

"See, I told you," he said, "I told you you took the wrong road."

Lofty knocked on the door, came in and asked for a cigarette.

"Looking a bit glum, A-ram," he said, a cheerful Cockney twinkle in his nose. He sat down and poured himself a cup of tea. He smelled like a mixture of sweat and cheese.

He always seemed content. I had seen him stand in the rain and the cold waiting for one of us to let him in, hungry and sick, sleeping in the basement like a dog in an alley, or in need of cigarettes which he seemed to need more than food, but never in any way unhappy, anxious, the least bit melancholy. I wondered if they gave him a lobotomy in the hospital. But he was always so full of energy, and talked like a nineteenth century raconteur in the backwoods of America. How did he get that way?

He made me feel worse. Ashamed of myself and helpless. Goddammit, I thought, if he can do it I can do it.

"What you need is a bit of chicken," he said, trying to read my mind. "A nice tart, that's what you need. Eh, A-ram, a little bit of the old business?"

"How d'you guess?"

"It's what we all need now, isn't it?" He said the last two words in two syllables as if he were clearing his throat.

He was not my idea of a father figure—and yet why not?

He dribbled tea on his stubbled chin and smiled at me through a face contorted by who knows how many shock treatments. And I thought of what the butcher around the corner told me about him, the plane in which he was a bombardier burning in a field in France, and the hospital, and coming home to find his wife and children gone. Dear Lofty and our common heritage.

"Okay, Lofty," I said, "I'll find one. A beautiful young woman."

"Good," he said, as if he were my father.

Her name was Anita but I called her Rosie.

In the saloon half of a working-class pub on Hampstead Road, old men playing Shove Ha'penny and darts on the other side of the wall, a bunch of us from school sat around a table and I stared at her when she wasn't looking. We were listening to the man she was with, sitting next to her, as he developed an argument, articulating with the polish of an onion something about a film we had just seen at the Everyman. He seemed confident in his thick turtleneck sweater, his lower lip protruding from the stem of a big pipe which implied a profound and heavy intelligence; he spoke in paragraphs with careful punctuation. I listened hard, squirming in the small black chair near the fireplace. She however seemed indifferent and with a soft backward wave of her hand smoothed her deep hair free and long behind her delicate neck. At moments she would catch my eyes and smile inquisitively. I wondered if it was because of my clothes, my nose, or the comments I would interject now and then.

Later I found out it was because of my "style": she had never known an American before.

By "style" she did not mean my accent but some peculiar way about me that she couldn't explain, and I thought of Yero with a cigar in his mouth. Of Marlon Brando. Of Gary Cooper. Groucho Marx. Huntz Hall.

"Is it good or bad?"

"Bad," she said, teasing me. But I was serious.

And so began the adventure of the Yank and the English girl.

But she wasn't a girl, and that was what I had to learn: that somewhere along the way we became men and women, whether I liked it or not.

Anita Spain. A strange name: she didn't know where it came from, assumed it was from the Armada, but in any case her people were English from way back. I called her Rosie thinking of Renoir's women whom she reminded me of. That was after she started coming to my place. Coming from the Vale of Heath and the quaint green quiet of ducks and sensuous willow caressing the lake, coming in cashmere and tweed sometimes and sometimes in bright Carnaby Street pop, down and out to Spitalfields and the brussel sprouts and tomatoes stinking rotten in the gutter, the meth-drinkers dribbling at her, coming up the broken stairs, undressing, leaving her expensive clothes on the dusty rug, watching me take off my old-man's long johns, the kind with the buttoned assflap reminding her of her grandfather in Wessex.

Partly because of the cold, partly because it was comfortable, but also because I was stingy and terribly afraid to appear well-dressed, I often dressed like a ragman, all bundled up in old clothes I bought at the flea market. She tried to change all that and secretly I wanted her to. But I put up a strong fight.

Why I attracted her I didn't really know except that she said that I was different and she never knew anyone like me before.

"And because you look good," she said, mimicking my speech. "I like your face."

128

It was a bright Saturday afternoon and we were walking down Portobello Road in Notting Hill Gate past the antique shops and the junk stalls. It was the year when young people in London began collecting old clothes and junk, assimilating remnants of the past, patching them up to form new styles different and unique and free of the drab gray fashions of their parents. Bright colors and wild shapes of the crowd flowed through the street and looking different was no longer a threat or a danger but common, just as common as Yero ever wanted to be. I began to feel at ease and not at all out of place or rebellious. But dressed in brown and black I still had a long way to go to join them.

Anita herself in lavender and jonquil was right at home with the sun and the time.

She was a beautiful young woman, olive complexion and soft dark eyes, long deep hair, and a figure drawn as if in my most pleasant dreams, full and warm. I was very proud of her and at first could not understand why she chose me for I did not feel at all worth her loveliness.

In those first few weeks I was very happy and followed her into the labyrinth of her whims: hither-thither she toured me through the spring's first flowers and the multicolored array of Saturday's leisure, the sun-soaked crowd of market people in Camden Town, concert people at Festival Hall, dinner people in Soho, pub people all over London; we must have met enough people to fill an auditorium for her songs, Spanish songs, Irish songs, French songs, even American songs she sang to herself while I stood drink in hand awk-

wardly in her shadow, drunk in the corner subdued by
her energy.

And I thought I could use her to save me. . . .

From my monster.

Woman: the warm broad expanse wide to my em-
brace, my eyes buried safe in the cuneiform secrets of
her night. Naked in the night and deep inside her I
would need no disguise to hide me from my monster.

I could escape in her arms. In the odor of her hair,
bury my face between her legs and taste that refuge,
primeval, viscous and deep, exuding as if from the lips
of ocean flowers, deep in a dark paradise. An elysium of
thick colors in soft shapes, orange and burnt sienna,
bright blue and animals, tigers, buffalo and flamingos
quiet and peaceful in the wide shade of huge banyan
trees of the kind I saw where?

I never saw a banyan tree in my life and yet there in
the winsome smile of her lust ripe figs and lichee nuts,
mangoes and kumquats would cover my face with the
pleasure of . . .

What?

What was pleasure?

I tried to use her as if she could teach me. Envi-
sioned myself lying on a magic carpet, my head resting
in my hand, elbow buried in a silk pillow, under fruit
blossoms, an exotic bird whistling in the branch, and
my Rosie peeling honeysuckle, slipping the soft wand
from the petals, feeding my tongue with sweet tiny
drops of nectar. As if she could feed me pleasure.

Or I would learn it through her own: watching her
ogle at Italian pastry in Soho, then go inside and buy it,
eating the custard slowly, letting it circulate in her

mouth: or watching her dance in that pub on Whitechapel Road where they had a rock group Friday and Saturday nights, her arms out, head back, eyes halfclosed and her mouth open to the music: or any of the multitude of pleasures she seemed to enjoy, and walking next to her, sometimes by the Thames along the old East India Docks, somber and mysterious, or the quay across the water from the Houses of Parliament, or in Hampstead Heath across the hills, or in the West End down Tottenham Court Road looking at the people, holding her hand as if she were leading me, I tried to see through her eyes as if her vision excluded the monster lurking around the corner.

Because I was really afraid of pleasure. It had been for me not the ambrosia of honeysuckle but Joe and Tony around the corner making Cathleen give them a blowjob behind Sal's Garage one afternoon when coming home from school I saw her on her knees as they held her head and would not let her go. Pleasure was when in a fight I punched Jack Russo in the face and felt his nose mash under my fist. Pleasure was the rage in football breaking that halfback's rib as he came around end, feeling the bone crack under my helmet. It was to be forgotten, buried in the past with those twenty Turks who raped Miss Berberian, the old lady with rabbit eyes, white silky hair, childless, barren now sitting quiet on her porch contemplative as an idiot, because when she was a small girl in Urfa twenty Turks fucked her crazy, ripped her inside out, and left her gagged with semen. I winced at pleasure catching myself in daydreams of the pleasure of a Southern white man dragging his choice slave girl into the woods, or the pleasure of S.S. doctors experimenting as boys do with frogs pulling their legs off and sticking them with pins with the delicious sound of the tight skin releasing blood—*Piff!*

And even deeper pleasure was my own skull smashed by a butcher's mallet, body sliced open from neck to groin, eyes plucked, tongue torn from its roots, and my carcass hung from a spike on a telephone pole: for how many times did I wish my face birthmarked purple, my legs shriveled by polio, or my brain swallowed by a tumor, that I might have an honorable justifiable cause for my own senseless suffering: how many times did I pray for a war that I might have a chance to vent my hatred and be killed for it: or wish for another Depression and the gaunt grimace of its hunger.

That was what pleasure became since . . . I couldn't remember differently unless I went way back . . . past the years of a long history . . . all the shit piled on top of my life by . . .

Who?

My country? Myself?

And my mother?

Of course my mother but that was too deep to understand.

But Anita would help me. She would get me back there. Past . . .

What did I do when Papa had a stroke, Ma?

I was driving her to Yero's. She was looking out the window.

I don't remember, she said easily.

Voyages

Did you take me to the hospital when you went to pick him up?

No, I left you downstairs with Mrs. Del Purgatorio.

What did I say when you brought him home?

I don't remember. I wasn't paying any attention to you then.

And how long and how often, I asked myself, because you were a tortured woman, did you not pay attention to me, Ma?

To the pleasure of my mother. My sweet mother. Past abandonment. Anita would take me back.

As if she were my angel.

As if I could be her child, holding her in the night.

As if she were more than herself, traveling her own long serpentine road of hidden destinations.

As if I could drag her down to my sadness, hook onto her neck and have her pull me out of my past.

Redeem me.

As if she were more than . . . I couldn't see beyond my needs so how could I describe her. . . . Age 25, brown eyes, brown hair, 120 pounds, left-handed, born and raised in a village in Surrey, mother died when she was ten, father became an alcoholic, older brothers took care of her, went to a Girl's Grammar and then on to university in London, first sexual intercourse at nineteen, liked to wear her hair long, worried about her teeth, was sloppy about the garbage and left vegetable peelings in the sink, smoked a few cigarettes a day rolling her own with licorice paper and Old Holborn tobacco, loved Thomas Hardy and Leo Tolstoi, Matisse, Bach and Ali Akbar Khan, enjoyed sex more than any-

133

thing else, worried about a little flabbiness in her belly, taught in an elementary school in Islington which made her feel important and secure, lived with another woman in Hampstead, decorated her room with children colors, reproductions of Matisse and Gauguin, a neat bookcase of paperbacks, a room all to herself, alone, afraid of spiders because of a childhood experience with a big spider caught in her hair, alone, cried for her mother sometimes at night, alone, hated her father and loved him and pitied him, alone, needed someone deeply, painfully sometimes because she felt alone, wanted a baby someday because why she didn't know and thought it might be instinctive or could it be because she felt alone, needed a man, someone who was strong, whom she could lean on sometimes when she felt alone. . . .

A *man* . . .

I wasn't, didn't want to be.

"Aram," she said, "stop putting yourself down. Please stop putting yourself down."

We were lying under an elm in a secluded corner of the Heath listening to a multitude of birds in the green glitter of the low sun in the early evening; we had just had a curry dinner in an Indian restaurant and had walked over to the Heath before going to a pub for some drinks. The dissonance of the birds, their various tunes mixed together, cheeps, chirps, pitched shrill and sweet, filled the space in my head and I became sad with their beauty, with Anita so beautiful, her hair and eyes soft in the slant of light, and I felt unequal to all that surrounded me.

"You're not," she said. "You're a *man*. You're a *good* man."

She had said this before, each time making me realize that what she saw in me was only what she wanted, needed: my silence had become a strength, my sensitivity a virtue, my baldness a sign of virility, my gentleness a grace rather than an awkwardness. But all this began to change as I dragged her down to my diffidence.

"And I'm a *woman*," she said, almost defiantly as if I had challenged her in some way. "I'm worth something, Aram."

"I know you are," I said, but she looked past me, as if she didn't hear.

"And I won't be made to feel worthless," she said. "I'm important and if I'm important then you must be also or why would I be with you?"

I didn't answer.

"I won't be made to feel worthless," she said.

"You're not worthless, Rosie. Nobody said you were."

"And I'm going to make it, Aram," she said, not to me but someone, anyone standing next to me or behind me, out there.

"I'm going to make it in this world," she said, off by herself now where I couldn't reach her anymore, way off, alone, with more fear than determination in her eyes.

It got cold. The sun was down, the sky red and purple behind the city. We walked to the pub, the amber streetlamps vivid and mesmeric like ancient and precious globes shining in the blue twilight. When we got there we both wanted to sit by the fire because we felt chilled. I bought her a whisky and a bottle of stout for myself. It was a large pub but quiet and not too many people there yet because it was early. I tried to talk to her about the film we had seen that afternoon but she didn't respond and after another round of drinks we got up to go.

"I want to go home alone," she said. "I don't want to go to your place with you tonight."

"Okay," I said.

We walked to the tube station and there I tried to kiss her but she turned away. I watched her walk back toward her place until the elevator came and then I took it down to the tunnel.

It had lasted a month: from the night I first slept with her . . . a month of respite, escape, safe with each other as if the world out there could not touch us when we were together, a month of her face in the hair of my chest, my balls snug in her hand, her cunt warm and moist in my hand, in the sweet salt smell of our private jungle, night birds and animal music, of our own fuck, delirious, rapt in each other as if without end, we were together for a month, less than a month, three weeks and six days, whispering to each other in the night like children, twenty-seven days of . . .

Gone.

I called her and through the phone she said:

"It's not going to work, Aram."

"Let me see you, Rosie. I want to see you."

"What for?"

"I need to."

"What for?"

"Come on, Rosie, don't be like that. I want to see you."

"All right then, where shall we meet?"

"Why don't you come to my place?"

"No."

"Then in the park by Russell Square. I'll meet you by the fountain."

"At what time?"

"Around three?"

"Make it four."

"Okay."

She came at four-thirty. I had been there an hour, sitting on a bench, thinking of her, going up and down and around her body, yearning, waiting. Flowers . . . what kind were they—What are the names of those flowers, Rosie—yellow and blue, rejoiced in the garden: I had never felt an afternoon so beautiful before. When she arrived we both felt as if we had been separated for years. She was more beautiful than I had ever seen her before.

She did not want to cry. I was the one who cried and she became angry.

"Don't," she said.

"Listen, Rosie. You're my last chance. I need you."

"I can't, Aram. I can't give you what you need. I have my own needs."

"Rosie."

"Oh, stop it, Aram!"

It felt good to make her angry. Her eyes were so far away and it was only when I made her angry that I could reach her somehow. But it was a dangerous touch, and she retreated even further.

There was nothing to say. It was not words I needed from her now but her lips, again, affirmative, as if she were my guardian angel. She knew this and became hard, her lips tight as if to say no to everything. For what she needed from me now was not my kiss, not anything I could give her, but my independence: a revolution in my life that would tear me from her power: she wanted me to blow my life apart so that never again would I need her to be my angel, my mother, or my dictator.

"I need you to be strong," she said. "I can't make it with you if you're not."

"Is it only my responsibility?"

"No, I must be strong, too. But I'm not. Not yet."

"And we can't help each other?"

"No. Not out there," she said, pointing to the sky as if there were planes overhead, bombers, helicopters dropping tear gas. "Not out there."

Where my monster . . .

We would see each other again but it would take a while, a long while, for the wounds to heal and . . .

"By that time I hope you change," she said, "I hope we both change."

And the wounds become scars.

Engraved behind our eyes.

Forever.

I panicked. I could not let her go. I wanted to hold on.

To whom? The woman who sat beside me, disgust in her eyes for my own tears? Wearing a pretty orange and yellow dress, her long brown hair, chestnut in the light, flowing behind her shoulders, who moved further and further away as I pleaded to let me hold her, desperately begged her to stay with me, stand by me? With the woman who lost respect for me as I sank deeper into my childhood?

With the child herself, crying for her mother? With the girl who was afraid of weakness, in herself and in others . . . in her father, her miserable father drunk like the bums in Spitalfields we used to see together, walking past them, and she would stare at them with horrible fascination?

Hold on, as if together, naked in the night, we could face the horrible black that would swallow us, each of us, alone.

"When am I going to see you again?"

"I don't know," she said. "I don't think I want to see you before the plane leaves. Are you still going?"

"No, I guess not."

"Then we'll probably see each other again in the fall."

She would be going to America for the summer. Her charter flight would be leaving in the next month. I was to go with her. I was going to show her around. And maybe pay her back in a way, as if I owed her pleasures in return for her love. I was going to take her places, show off my knowledge: it was my country, after all, MY country, and who should know it better than I: as if I were proud of it. For did I not attract her because of my style?

And oh there was so much more I was going to do with her, as if I could change! And experiment. All the different places of our lives we hadn't yet explored. And the mysteries. All the secrets of our lives we could discover together. Strange places we would travel without fear or loneliness. Hotel rooms we could share for the price of one. Films we wouldn't have to go to when we could entertain each other walking in the streets.

Come back to me, Rosie. Please. Let me know the pleasure of your sighs again, my cock deep inside you, that I may taste you, taste you.

And all that I would have offered her, all the beautiful talents inside me I could give her if she dug deep enough.

Enter me, Rosie, come inside me and bring me out of myself.

And what she would have offered me, her face in the morning, every morning, knowing she would be there always, in the night.

We were going to be happy together.

Happy.

Home in the country.

Children.

Gone.

No, not gone.

Not gone, Rosie. Anita. My love.

"That's not what you want to hold on to," she said. I almost didn't hear her.

"Look at me, Aram. Look at *me*."

"Rosie."

"My name isn't Rosie."

I couldn't see her. Only the rejection. The loss of . . . what?

"I'm not your past," she said. "I'm not your ancient city by the river, your strawberry ice-cream, your father's hands, your . . ."

"I know. I know."

"Then change."

"How?"

"I don't know. It's hard enough for me alone."

Alone. Each of us. Separate. In our own separate cars in the night, following little red lights as when driving across country, nothing ahead and nothing behind us.

"I'm going," she said. "I'm not rejecting you, I'm just going."

And she walked away and did not turn around. The five o'clock crowd filled the streets and covered her up. I walked with it in the opposite direction toward Charing Cross Station. But I didn't want to go back to my house so I continued walking, crossed the bridge and walked through the pavilion of the Festival Hall and then came back across the Waterloo Bridge and then walked to the Bank and there finally hopped a bus back to Spitalfields.

I called her twice after that. The second time she didn't even get angry but asked me to take care of myself.

And it was over.

England is as far north as the snow in Canada where the Eskimos live in igloos. And yet its weather is not at all as inclement as that of New York's much farther south, its winters not half as cold, and from spring to fall there are many days when you can sunbathe in London and need only a light jacket at night. The parks are full of people then, everyone enjoying the air still warm from the Caribbean. Such were the days after she left and Whitsuntide came with a burst of sun. Without her I went into the summer feeling sorry for myself, strolling through the streets she taught me, back to all the places she brought alive. Hands in my pockets I smiled sadly at men and women who looked happy together: Listen, I told them under my breath, I was with a woman once, too.

She sent me postcards signed in bright colors: Cheers, Anita.

I couldn't write her back because she was always moving around. Postcards came from all over the country, my country: she was sending it back to me. She even went to see Yero and Melina.

Dear Aram, she wrote in swift smooth letters, it's really amazing how alike you and your brother are. . . . Your mother is a darling and I wish I could have spent more time with her.

The coincidence of the different parts of my life seemed unreal: the categories I had molded and hardened for so many years began falling apart, mixing together into a thick inchoate puddle of emotions I had to examine all over again. Postcards came from all her new pleasures: enjoying even the jungle heat of New York, her legs dangling from a fire escape at midnight in the Lower East Side, she watched Puerto Rican urchins below dancing between the garbage cans, and I saw her with all the pleasures I had once ignored, watermelon and corn, a warm rain in Central Park, sunset on the waterfront; she was sending them back to me.

I love you, Anita.

How much? Enough to leave her alone? She had her own life to lead.

And I mine. Yet I was not any better, and in the night cried out to her with the fear that I would never see her again, never taste her nipples again, the soft wet lips of her cunt.

In September, I hoped, I will see her in September; September is a good time to start all over.

But when she wrote of hitchhiking with a new friend whom she didn't name I fell down again, deeper this time, crying from my gut, hating her with a jealousy I had never known before . . . never unless I went back, way back to something I had lost and would never have again.

Bitch!

Warm syrupy pain flowed through the hollow of my neck, spread and seeped through the convolutions of my brain: thoughts led nowhere, coiled among themselves like insects: she never loved me, she never loved me.

"Do try and be happy," she wrote, "my darling."

I'm not your darling, you filthy douche bag.

And each day I waited for another card and when none came my hatred sank deeper and deeper until by the middle of summer I gave up all hope.

It seemed that all my pain would never make any difference.

Would I ever get better?

Fog filled the streets, spreading miasmic with the stench of bacteria from the Truman's Brewery in Bethnal Green. I felt as if I had lost myself, and searched my rooms for some kind of strength, something to hold on to, only to find bobby pins and long hairs. She was not really gone, not inside me, not as long as I was alive; not unless someone cut her out of my brain or burned her away with some fine instrument of modern science, and then it would have to burn all the rest of it too: my father's horrible twisted mouth, my mother crying in my arms, and even deeper to blood in the sand, pieces of flesh left to the worms; not unless it burned deep behind my eyes or sliced a final irredeemable line through my brain so that I could live the rest of my life like a vegetable, a silent hulk in the corner.

Either I was going to live with her in peace or I would go on hating her for the rest of my life, and it wasn't really her I hated.

Beautiful Anita. If not an angel, certainly a very beautiful woman.

So I came home one night after a bath around the corner and made myself a big meal of bulghur and lamb chops I bought from the Cypriot on Brick Lane. Lofty came up for dessert and we drank Turkish coffee, which he didn't like— "Bit like mud, isn't it?" he said— and we smoked cigarettes and then he left. I was going to read but instead I started looking in the mirror. I had a very unusual face, even by Armenian standards, and I began entertaining myself with a long repertoire of masks I developed over the years: satanic, cherubic, but mostly ridiculous: the awesome Turk, the poor hobo, the tired old man, the great maestro . . . and then I took a break. The muscles above my eyes and in my jaw relaxed and there was no expression at all in the face in the mirror.

I stared curiously.

It was a gentle face, good, innocent, sad but beautiful and suddenly all the love I ever wanted from Anita, from anyone, came out of me for myself.

Wherever she was, I hoped she was happy.

Son, my father said, America is a nightmare from which we are struggling to awake.

He sat across the table in Lofty's chair, his bald head resplendent in the shafts of morning light.

Wisdom was too hard to come by. Imagination was all I could manage. With the help of others. He looked at me through the eyes of Rembrandt.

But we will wake, he said, one morning we'll hear the ragman sing, see him dance in the street.

What should I do in the meanwhile, Papa?

Wander and search, he said, wander and search.

I didn't like that answer but I had only myself to blame.

I thought of going to Turkey but it was too far and expensive. And anyway I wasn't looking for roots anymore: the bones were buried too far deep and wouldn't, I finally realized, do me any good.

So I went to France. Then Spain. And the wonders therein.

But I was tired. And everything was so expensive. And Paris and Madrid were not at all the way Hemingway described them.

My money ran out in Madrid and I had just enough left for a few more hotel rooms and the ticket from Paris to Dover. But I had to give up the hotel rooms because hitchhiking in Spain was too hard so I took the third class to San Sebastian. Hitchhiking up from the border I almost told the people who picked me up that I was English. I had been ashamed of being American for so long that it seemed a great relief to be in a country where I could pass for someone else. But the first time I considered doing that I thought of my brother. It wasn't that I owed any allegiance to imitation hamburgers and orange drink and everything else back there that I hated and would always hate, but I missed him, I missed him a lot, not his way of life, but something I left back there that I never came to grips with. I remembered the night I left. Everyone else stayed at his house and he drove me to the airport. It was a beautiful night, clean and cold and a full moon rising over Brooklyn. He was almost as excited as I was.

"Try and make it to Italy," he said. "I had a ball in Italy."

"What did you do there?"

"Everything."

"Nice women?"

"Not only the women. The people. My buddy was Italian. We went everywhere. It was great. Really great. I never made it to England, though. I'd like to see England."

He carried my bag to the terminal. I walked a step behind him and for one quick moment felt how good it would be if I could give him the trip and let him go over there and enjoy it, almost as if I were his older brother.

"Don't forget now," he said importantly, "keep your passport with you no matter what. Your passport is everything. Without it you're nobody."

After I checked in we went up to the lounge and he

bought me a bourbon and a scotch for himself. It made him feel good to buy me a drink just as it would make me feel good to buy him one. We sat at a small round table and watched the other people and didn't say anything to each other. And then I bought another round. And then he bought a round and we both started to feel it. I never got loaded with him before except once at a wedding and then we weren't really together with all the other people around. He got very happy when he was drunk. I wondered what he'd be like with marihuana and asked him if he ever tried it.

"It gave me a headache," he said.

"Too bad."

"I don't need it."

"I guess not."

"Do you smoke it a lot?"

"Sometimes."

"Just don't get caught."

"No. No reason why I should."

"You never know."

I would've liked to turn him on. Maybe someday, I thought. Then my flight was called on the speaker.

He carried my bag down the corridor and I got out my ticket for the girl at the gate. When we reached her he said for the hundredth time:

"You got everything now? You didn't forget anything? Well, if you did, we can send it to you." He was very nervous.

I kept smiling and smiling, nervously. I wanted to kiss him and hug him but I couldn't.

"Okay," he said and patted my shoulder. "See you next year maybe, eh?"

"Sure."

"Take it easy, kid."

"You too, Yero."

It was the first time I ever called him by his name. I was the first to turn and walk away.

I knew he'd be up there to watch the plane take off. When I got outside and walked to the plane the wind blew hard and cold. I turned to see him up above but it was too dark and I couldn't find him. I waved in the direction that I thought he was in. I was crying a little bit. It felt good.

He was back there. In the darkness. I waved to him: See you later, Yero. But no answer came out of the night. I wasn't too far from Bordeaux but it was too late to get a ride and I went to sleep in some woods by a river. It was a warm night and no need for a hotel. The stars reminded me of Texas of all places, I didn't know why: memories mingled in crazy patterns and all parts of the world were related. The bread and the cheese and the wine of course was like nothing you could get in America, but the stars were always the same. I slept for a couple of hours and then it was light. When I woke the dawn was a very soft red and an easy blue with a spot of silver from the morning star. I tried to stay awake because the sky was so beautiful but I was very tired, and as I let my head sink back in my duffel and closed my eyes I was glad I woke when I did: it was very important to keep that image of the red sky locked behind my eyes so that I would always have it with me no matter what, always so that if I ever thought about sui-

cide I could hold on to it. It seemed wrong somehow
that Hemingway killed himself at dawn. Dawn came
and the sun streamed out and he turned around and
went right back into the night, the black, where there is
nothing, not even pain. Shotgun at dawn, the barrels
pressed above his eyes, thumbs flipping each trigger.
. . . As if he could escape into the bosom of the light.
That was in America. In Montana. Of the big sky. Did
we share, I wondered, the same monster?

It took all day to get to Paris. By the time I reached
there I had no money left for anything to eat and my
train wouldn't be leaving for another three hours. It was
night and it began to drizzle and everything looked
ugly. I tried to sleep in the station but I was too tired,
too tense, and it was too uncomfortable on the bench, so
I walked around the city some more.

I was tired.

I was very tired.

I wanted to go home.

Where? Anywhere.

The monster was everywhere: strangers walked past
me, around me, through me, through each other, bump-
ing each other, avoiding each other, touching, afraid to
touch, pushing, shoving, opening the door politely, tip-
ping hats, snarling through their teeth. . . .

I wanted to go home and take a bath and go to bed.
In the morning I would sing and be happy.

The city roared. What city? Where was I? But what
difference did it make? The monster would never go
away. There was no running away. It killed and
maimed and tortured and would live forever, would
never die. . . .

In the night. . . .

Unless I could find out what it looked like and stare in its eyes and squeeze it by the throat and kill it and bury it and carve its picture on my hands, incised deep across the lines of my fortune.

I'm not going to be crippled, Papa!

My son, he said, I never wanted you to be. Why did you think I did?